THE CHURCH AS THE
SURROGATE FAMILY

Robbie Edwards Mills

WestBow
PRESS
A DIVISION OF THOMAS NELSON

WestBow Press books may be ordered through booksellers or by contacting:

WestBow Press
A Division of Thomas Nelson
1663 Liberty Drive
Bloomington, IN 47403
www.westbowpress.com
1-(866) 928-1240

Because of the dynamic nature of the Internet, any web addresses or links contained in this book may have changed since publication and may no longer be valid. The views expressed in this work are solely those of the author and do not necessarily reflect the views of the publisher, and the publisher hereby disclaims any responsibility for them.

Any people depicted in stock imagery provided by Thinkstock are models, and such images are being used for illustrative purposes only.

Certain stock imagery © Thinkstock.

ISBN: 978-1-4497-2660-7 (sc)
ISBN: 978-1-4497-2659-1 (e)

Library of Congress Control Number: 2011916404

Printed in the United States of America

WestBow Press rev. date: 11/17/2011

CONTENTS

ABSTRACT

This project presents a practical theology model for nurturing rural African Methodist youth, using the church as a surrogate family. Oak Chapel African Methodist Episcopal Church moved from a struggling traditional congregation to this surrogate family model, and it reduced conflict and enhanced cooperation in the church. This practical theology model provided seven theme sermons on the attributes of God and his family to provide a spiritual foundation for church youth. Seven African style intergenerational Bible studies were created to facilitate healing, sustaining, guiding, and reconciling with Jesus the Christ; the studies were needed to counteract some of the effects of poverty, racism, and nihilism that is prevalent in the community. The implementation of this holistic model resulted in enhanced confidence, spiritual growth, and maturity among the youth and increased growth in the church family.

ACKNOWLEDGMENTS

We are thankful for the opportunity to be a part of the Practical Theology for Pastors, Chaplains, and Clinicians track at Wesley Theological Seminary. I am deeply grateful to the faculty and staff who assisted me in broadening my horizons. A word of thanks to Rebecca Scheirer, who was always there with an encouraging word and who made our civil rights immersion one of the most memorable experiences of our lives. A special thanks to Dr. Lew Parks, who saw beneath the superficial to guide me to do the project that was God's will. I want to express a special note of gratitude to Dr. Michael Koppel, who was both a track leader and the reader for the project; I would like to express my sincere appreciation for his cyber inspiration, kindness, guidance, and challenges to go deeper in my analysis.

A special thanks to my husband, Clark, who traveled with me to each of the classes and provided much-needed suggestions and encouragement. Thank you for all your support in my ministry and educational endeavors. You have been my constant companion and friend, challenging my thought process and actions throughout the project. Without your support and encouragement, I would not have achieved this milestone in my life.

I want to express deep gratitude to Reverend Evelyn Gail Dunn, the presiding elder of the Southern District of the North Carolina Conference of the AME Church. Reverend Dunn provided a listening ear to many of my wandering thoughts and gave spiritual mentoring throughout my ministry and this project. She always provided enlightenment and helped me to proceed forward with greater confidence. I also want to thank her for allowing me to do my presentation at the Southern District Conference. She has been such a blessing to me and my ministry.

I must give a word of thanks to Whitney and Meghan Mills, who typed much of the project and provided me technical support. A huge thanks to all my classmates, Kelley Mills, Dr. Jamie Mills, Anne Mulder, Larrenda Graham, and Stephon Mills, for all your support and help. I would like to thank Bishop and Mrs. Adam Jefferson Richardson, Jr., for believing in my ministry and providing financial support through the Nehemiah Ministry to restore Oak Chapel AME Church. Your smiles and encouragement have been a real blessing to us. Thank you for having the courage to appoint me to Oak Chapel and give me an opportunity to serve the wonderful people of Warren County.

I would like to thank my presiding elder, Larry S. Hinton, and Mrs. Hinton for their financial contribution to Oak Chapel and their guidance and support throughout my four years there. I am deeply appreciative of the ministerial staff, officers, and members at Oak Chapel for their cooperation and service during my absences and for their partnership on this project.

I would also like to express sincere appreciation to my coworkers, who have fulfilled my obligations at the office in my absences. Thank you for your input and assistance. Without your support and technical assistance, this achievement would not have been possible. I want to express my genuine gratitude to Jackie Alston, Jonathan Winstead, Glynis Edmonds, and Elsie McFarland. We give God all the glory for his salvation and abundant life.

INTRODUCTION

This work will explore the church as a surrogate family. The context is a small African Methodist Episcopal Church (AMEC) in a small town in northeastern North Carolina. The project was conducted at the Oak Chapel AME Church. The historic church was founded 145 years ago. Newly freed slaves needed a place where they could worship. They had been attending churches founded by slaveholders. These churches allowed African Americans to worship in the balcony and in the back of the church when balconies were nonexistent. This setup was uncomfortable and inconvenient for them. In 1866, several families joined together under the inspiration of God and founded a church where they could worship with freedom and dignity.

In the 140th year of the church's existence, I was appointed pastor. As my family and I traveled back home from the North Carolina Annual Conference, the Holy Spirit whispered to my spirit that the church should be "a healing center." On the first Sunday of the new conference year, no one came to worship at our church. Three weeks later, an elderly member died. She was the only known member of the church. Therefore, the first year there was much physical and spiritual rehabilitation that had to be done in order to establish a viable congregation.

In the second year of my pastorate, some children and youth started attending church services. God provided a van to transport them to church services twice a week. Most of the youth had not been active in church activities prior to attending Oak Chapel. They enjoyed gathering at the church for Bible study, Sunday school, and worship services. Many of the youth became active members of the church even though their parents did not attend. They traveled out of town to church conferences and other youth activities without their parents.

What emerged at Oak Chapel AME Church was a surrogate family model. The children and youth sought out church leaders for guidance and direction for their needs, concerns, and life issues. Many of their parents had to work long hours for low wages just to provide the basic necessities. These working parents were not able to accompany their children to church. The informal and indirect family surrogate model developed into a formal and direct one in the summer of 2010.

I realized that Jesus created a surrogate model when he began his ministry with a group of disciples. Jesus left the family of his birth and became an itinerant preacher who met the needs of those who crossed his path. As people were healed and delivered, they followed him so they could come to know God, the Father. They saw God in action in the person of Jesus as they walked and talked in this new community. Jesus provided the model for the church. He re-enacted the family surrogate model for the future church, so they could develop a similar model in every community on the planet. In the family of God, the spiritual family would take priority over the biological family.

The family surrogate model is an expression of the real church. This model possesses contagious love that nurtures and supports others in the family of God. There is commitment, loyalty, and faithfulness to God and his family. Just as Jesus and his disciples honored the truth of Scriptures, the model church teaches honesty and justice in all dealings. The sharing of material resources was evident in the community Jesus created and continued in the early first-century church. The disciples of Jesus were unified and enjoyed fellowship with one another. Jesus and his disciples honored God with worship and lived moral lives. The themes of love, loyalty, honesty, giving or sharing of material resources, unity, fellowship, and holiness are pillars upon which the surrogate family model was developed at Oak Chapel AME Church.

Each month from June through December, one of these pillars was explored. I shared a sermon on the theme for that month as it related to the surrogate family model. I also did a Bible study or Family Fun Night centered around specific topics for each month. These studies were intergenerational, and the sharing of stories provided encouragement, support, and nurturing for the youth and children. The Family Fun Night gatherings were held outside the church on the lawn with chairs in a circle. Once the nights became too cool and too dark to meet outside, they took place in the church basement. The children played tribal drums for these services. Members learned to participate in the sharing and re-authoring of their own stories as a result of hearing biblical stories. The elders of the community encouraged the youth to voice their concerns and express their anxieties over future challenges. They learned that they are a part of the family of God with God as their father, Jesus as their brother, and the Holy Spirit as their guide.

When the project began on June 1, 2010, there were thirteen youths between the ages of six months and eighteen years of age. There were seven adults who were active in the church; four adults were semi-active in church activities. The leadership team consisted of three ministers, an ordained minister who was designated as children's minister, the pastor, and one additional minister, all of which were female. The three active adult males served as trustees and assisted with various church activities.

Before the surrogate family model was implemented, inappropriate interactions were common. Biological siblings would provide personal care and assistance for their own siblings and ignore the small children who did not have an older sibling. The smaller children would seek an adult to assist them when meals and snacks were being served. A few preschool children would ask to go in with an older sibling instead of volunteering to go to their own age-appropriate class.

At the beginning of the project, each person over the age of five responded to five statements to determine their relationship with the church family. Family boundaries were established, which awarded points for meritorious conduct and deducted points for inappropriate interactions. The church leaders implemented time out for preschoolers who were out of the family boundaries. The first Bible study taught that all people in the church were siblings, since they were a part of God's family. They were taught to serve all preschoolers at the same time, since they were all siblings. An emphasis on calling each other brother and sister was reinforced.

As the surrogate family model and the undergirding themes were taught, the teens led the preschoolers in developing posters and banners. They expressed how they viewed the various themes using pictures and diagrams. The Sunday school teachers would highlight the themes in the lessons, as well. The same occurred in the Bible studies that were being conducted on the book of Revelations. The Young Peoples Department (YPD) created banners to hang in the sanctuary for each of the themes.

The church leadership made encouragement, support, and nurturing the primary focus as they interrelated with the youth.

The goal of God's surrogate family is for the church to be a place where young people will be empowered to overcome the obstacles of success and not be encumbered by past experiences. They will hopefully grow and mature by following the model of Jesus used in helping his disciples develop healthy relationships. They will hopefully develop a positive self-image as they achieve the successful completion of life skills in a safe and secure environment. The family surrogate model will provide resources for holistic spiritual development which leads to mental and emotional maturity.

The introduction will provide an overview of the family surrogate model project. The context and setting will be discussed. The current conditions that were present at the time of the project will be described. An action plan that discusses the implementation of the model throughout the seven months will be provided. Before-and-after evaluation tools, which consist of observations, interviews, and surveys, will be noted.

The first chapter provides a historical perspective on the town of Warrenton, Warren County, Oak Chapel AME Church, and the African Methodist Episcopal Denomination. It focuses on the last 150 years. Chapter two details the theological component and past and contemporary exegesis of Scriptures reveals the family surrogate model. This chapter also examines the teachings of Jesus and Paul that emphasize the family of God as well as the theological themes characteristic of the spiritual family with a summary of the sermons and Bible Studies included.

The scholarly work of Joseph H. Hellerman, C. Anthony Hunt, Edward P. Wimberly, and Tapiwa N. Mucherera is summarized to provide a basis for the surrogate family model. The project seeks to determine what impact the family surrogate model will have on Oak Chapel African Methodist Episcopal Church in North Carolina. Chapter three provides the methodology used to come to this conclusion. Chapter four analyzes the observations, interviews, and surveys, and highlights changes that occurred between June and December 2010. Chapter five discusses the implications for further study and conclusions regarding the family surrogate model. Chapter six provides implications and reflections on the state of the church as a whole and my personal story.

CHAPTER ONE

HISTORY AND INFLUENCES OF POVERTY AND RACISM

Oak Chapel African Methodist Episcopal Church was founded in 1866 in Warrenton, North Carolina.[1] At that time in history, the town of Warrenton was a vibrant and bustling center of agribusiness. The history of the last 150 years could be described as a tale of two cities; the town of Warrenton and the county of Warren was a prominent center of agriculture, architecture, education, and social hospitality in 1860. In 1860 there were approximately 700 people in the town. In the year 2000 there were 811 people living in the boundaries of Warrenton. [2] How did the region grow to be a prominent center of agriculture, architecture, education, and social hospitality?

First let us look at the beginning of Warren County. In 1765 the area that is now known as Warren County was a part of Bute County, which was named after John Stuart, Third Earl of Bute, the British Prime Minister, and Lord of the Treasury. In 1779, during the fourth

---

[1]   Ada Strong Johnson, *An Historical Sketch of the Oak Chapel African Methodist Episcopal Church of Warrenton, North Carolina* (Warrenton, NC: Jennie A, Johnson Franklin, 2007), 12.

[2]   Carey Aselage, Arlana Bobo, Aviva Meyer, Betsy Neal, and Katie Parker, "Warrenton, Warren County, NC: *A Community Diagnosis Including Secondary Data Analysis and Qualitative Data Collection*," April 2001, http://www.hsl.unc.edu/phpapers/warrentonol/whistory.htm. (Accessed Jan. 3, 2011.)

year of the American Revolution, a group of patriots petitioned the North Carolina Assembly to divide Bute County into two separate counties. The southern portion of Bute became Franklin County to honor Benjamin Franklin. The northern portion was named after Dr. Joseph Warren, a physician who had been killed at Bunker Hill during the American Revolution.[3]

Thomas and William Christmas sold one hundred acres of land to the town of Warrenton on July 22, 1779, and drew up the first plan for the town. Warrenton became the county seat for Warren County.[4] The county flourished due to its plantation slave system economy. Free labor from Africa planted, cultivated, and harvested tobacco and later cotton. As a result of the abundant resources of land and free labor, the county and town grew prosperous, influential, and wealthy. Warren County became the wealthiest county in North Carolina by 1860.[5]

The majority of slaves worked in the fields from dawn to dusk. The aristocracy enjoyed music, dance, and elegant dinners. The male patriarchs pursued horse breeding and racing, and the children of the plantation owners attended the Warrenton male and female academies with similar youth from around the state. Three major hot spring resorts located in the county attracted people from the East Coast; people believed the hot springs had healing properties, and the elite would come to bathe in hope of restoration. The popular resort hotels provided rest, relaxation, and an opportunity to be enriched by the liberal arts available as entertainment.[6]

In the early eighteenth century, people built numerous churches throughout the county, and Warrenton was no exception.[7] Some of these Warrenton churches had balconies where the African slaves were

---

[3] Town of Warrenton, *"Historic Warrenton North Carolina,"* Http:www. warrenton-NC.com/history.shtml. (Accessed Jan. 3, 2011).

[4] Ibid.

[5] Ibid.

[6] Aselage et al., *"A Community Diagnosis,"* www.hsl.unc.edu/phpapers/ warrentonol/whistory.htm. (Accessed Jan. 3, 2011.)

[7] Lizzie Wilson Montgomery, *Sketches of Old Warrenton, North Carolina* (Spartanburg, SC: The Reprint Company Publishers, 1984), 170-208.

allowed to sit.[8] According to Albert S. Raboteau, there were mixed but segregated congregations throughout the south before slavery ended in both the Baptist and Methodist churches. He states that those churches allowed slaves and free black people to sit in the back pews when the church did not have a gallery.[9] Those conditions limited the slaves' ability to be true participants in church worship services.

The ruling aristocracy controlled the churches, and slaves were not allowed to hold positions of leadership in the church. In 1832 North Carolina passed a law that barred slaves and free blacks from preaching or exhorting in public.[10] Raboteau states that Methodists licensed the black preachers as exhorters in an attempt to skirt North Carolina law. As a result of their courage, early black preachers gave birth to many Christian communities among slaves and free blacks. Bryant Rudd, who is the great, great uncle of my husband, was one of those black Methodist preachers in neighboring Halifax County.[11]

In 1840 workers completed the Raleigh and Gaston Railroad, which traveled through Warren County.[12] John A. Hyman was born as a slave near Warrenton in 1840 and was taught to read and write by his slave owner, who was a Pennsylvania jeweler named King. Hyman worked as a janitor until it was discovered that King had taught him how to read and write. King and his family were forced to leave Warrenton, and John Hyman was torn from his young family and sold as a slave to a new owner in Alabama. The Civil War ended in 1865, and Hyman returned to his family in Warrenton. [13]

---

[8]   Oral History provided by Rev. Tom Carlson, the current pastor of the Warrenton Presbyterian Church, 2009.

[9]   Albert J. Raboteau, *Slave Religion: The "Invisible Institution" in the Antebellum South*, updated edition (New York: Oxford University Press, 2004), 137.

[10]   Ibid., 135-137.

[11]   Ibid., 135-137.

[12]   Manly Wade Wellman, *The County of Warren North Carolina 1586-1917* (Chapel Hill, NC: The University of North Carolina Press, 1959), 116.

[13]   Deloris Williams, NC Gen Web Project, John A. Hyman Biography, August 21, 2010 http://www.Ncgenweb.us/Ncwarren/afro/hyman-ja.htm & Montgomery (Accessed Jan. 3, 2011), *Sketches of Old Warrenton*, 88-89.

In 1865 he became a delegate to the North Carolina Equal Rights Convention, which was held at St. Paul African Methodist Episcopal Church in Raleigh, North Carolina.[14] While serving as a delegate at the convention, Hyman was exposed to the great work of the AME Church in the areas of education and equal rights. These were two of his passions. In 1866 John Hyman set aside a portion of his homestead for the building of a basement that served as an African Methodist church and a Freedman's Bureau school for local African American children. Teachers from the North were sent to Warrenton to teach those who desired an education.[15]

History of Oak Chapel AME Church

In 1866 Bishop Alexander Wayman of the African Methodist Episcopal Church took a tour of the South from Richmond, Virginia, to Georgia, and his second stop was in Warrenton, North Carolina. His purpose was to assist and encourage the organizing of churches.[16] A group of concerned citizens of African American heritage in Warrenton and Warren County desired a place where they could worship in true freedom. They obtained permission to build a church for the purpose of continuing secular and religious education and providing worship services. Young families worked together to build a sanctuary, and later a parsonage, on the original lot donated by John A. Hyman.[17]

John Hyman developed and operated a store where newly freed slaves could buy goods and essential supplies for daily living. In 1868 he participated in a Constitutional convention and was elected a state senator. He served the region as a Republican senator until 1874. (Because Abraham Lincoln was a Republican, most black politicians became members of the Republican Party.) In 1874 Hyman was elected

---

[14]   Minutes of the Freedmen's Convention, Raleigh, NC, 1866, 3, 6. http:// docsouth.unc.edu/NC/freedmen (Accessed January 3, 2011).

[15]   Ada S. Johnson, *Oak Chapel History*, 5.

[16]   Charles Spencer Smith, *A History of the AME Church* (Philadelphia: Book Concern of AME Church, 1922), 64.

[17]   Ada S. Johnson, *Oak Chapel History*, 5.

to represent the Second Congressional District of North Carolina in the United States Congress. He was the first person of African ancestry that served as a member of the House of Representatives from the state of North Carolina. He served from 1875 to 1877 but was not reelected because of opposition from the white members of the Republican Party. They said that five thousand dollars per year was excessive for a "kinky head."[18]

From its beginning, Oak Chapel AME Church has nurtured, enlightened, enriched, and empowered local citizens. The church served both God and the community by providing a place of worship. The pastors and members were instrumental in the struggle for true equality and liberty. They fought for education, social justice, and the right to vote. The church was an anchor for the oppressed in Warrenton and Warren County. The families that founded the church were leaders in the community, state, and nation.

On April 8, 1867, Bishop Daniel Payne appointed Reverend William W. Morgan as the pastor of Oak Chapel African Methodist Church in Warrenton, North Carolina. The few existing AME churches in North Carolina were a part of the South Carolina Annual Conference, and this was the first pastoral appointment of record.[19] Oral history notes that a group of African Methodist believers had been meeting in homes and the church basement prior to April 8, 1867. One of the founding families of Oak Chapel was Ossian and Kitty Hawkins.[20] Ossian Hawkins became a Warren County commissioner in the 1870s.[21]

The first child of Ossian and Kitty was John R. Hawkins, who was also a charter member of Oak Chapel. He was born May 31, 1862, in Warrenton, North Carolina. He attended Hampton Institute in Hampton, Virginia, and returned to teach in the Warren County schools in 1878, becoming the principal of the elementary school

---

[18] Ginger Meek, *"Rich History of Church Source of Members' Pride"* in the *Warren Record Warrenton, NC*, August 1, 1990, 3.

[19] Charles S. Smith, *A History of the AME Church*, 517.

[20] Ada S. Johnson, *Oak Chapel History*, 6.

[21] Eric Anderson, *Race and Politics in North Carolina, 1872-1901: The Black Second*, (Baton Rouge: Louisiana State University Press, 1981), 54.

in 1880. He served as a professor of mathematics and business manager at Kittrell College in Kittrell, North Carolina, from 1884 until 1890, when he became the president of the college.[22] Kittrell was an African Methodist Episcopal Church college that was started on February 7, 1886, to provide education for African Americans because education at the secondary and college level was very limited.[23]

John R. Hawkins served as the president of Kittrell College until 1896. [24] Oak Chapel was the closest AME Church to Kittrell College, and many of the students and faculty attended worship services there. In 1869 the North Carolina Conference of the AME Church was started. Oak Chapel subsequently became an active member of the North Carolina Conference.[25] In 1896 John R. Hawkins was elected as the secretary of the department of education of the AME Church. He was married to the great granddaughter of Bishop Richard Allen, the founder of the AME Church.[26]

John R. Hawkin's wife was Lillian Marie Kennedy, who graduated from the Conservatory of Music in Philadelphia with honors. She came to Kittrell College to be the department head for the department of music in September of 1888. After her husband was elected to the secretary of the department of education for the AME Church, they relocated to Washington DC. John R. Hawkins continued in that position until 1912, when he was elected as the financial secretary of the AME Church. He received his law degree from Howard University in 1915.[27] Hawkins as a trustee became an

---

22   Richard R. Wright, Jr., and John R. Hawkins, editors, *Centennial Encyclopaedia of the African Methodist Episcopal Church* (Philadelphia: AME Church made available by UNC-Ch Library, Chapel Hill, NC), 357.

23   Charles S. Smith, *A History of the AME Church*, 85.

24   Wright & Hawkins, *Centennial Encyclopaedia*, 357-358.

25   Charles S. Smith, *A History of the AME Church*, 85

26   Wright & Hawkins, *Centennial Encyclopaedia*, 357-358.

27   Ibid.

incorporator of the AME Church in 1936.[28] He was active in the leadership of the AME Church, serving as financial secretary until his death in 1939.[29]

The church was located two blocks east of the center of town and the courthouse. A map of the town in 1882 located the church in the two block town commons. Oak Chapel was one of two churches that were identified as serving citizens of African ancestry; the Baptist church later moved to a different location. Oak Chapel has stood the test of time, remaining in its original building and original location.

Oak Chapel AME Church sits on a strong foundation of Methodism. In reality what is now known as the Methodist Church started as a "Holy Club" at Christ Church College in Oxford University in London, England. Two brothers were instrumental in the development of the Holy Club as a religious piety student movement. Charles Wesley, who is best known for his many hymns, and his brother John Wesley, who was a circuit rider traveling to preach an evangelical gospel, focused on holiness and spiritual disciplines. The new movement crossed the Atlantic Ocean in the 1730s and first put down roots in the northeast of the American colonies. Frances Asbury, Thomas Coke, and George Whitefield spread Methodism throughout the colonies.[30] In 1780, Bishop Frances Asbury brought the Methodist revival to Warren County, North Carolina.[31]

All who were converted under their preaching came together in 1784 to form the Methodist Episcopal Church. The Methodist movement was partially responsible for the period of intense revival in American called The First Great Awakening in the 1740s. John Wesley received black converts without reservation; he had previously

---

[28] *The Book of Discipline of the African Methodist Episcopal Church* (Nashville: AMEC Sunday School Union, 2009), 44.

[29] Richard R. Wright, Jr., ed., *Encyclopaedia of African Methodism* 2nd ed. (Philadelphia: The Book Concern of the AME Church, 1947), 582.

[30] C. Eric Lincoln and Lawrence H, Mamiya, *The Black Church in the African American Experience* (Durham, NC: Duke University Press, 1990), 49.

[31] Manly Wade Wellman, *The County of Warren North Carolina 1586-1917* (Chapel Hill, NC: The University of North Carolina Press, 1959), 62.

opposed slavery in England and continued to offer the right hand of fellowship to African Americans. When the first Methodist society was organized in Maryland, blacks were listed as charter members even though some of them were slaves.[32] In 1790, approximately 20 percent of the membership of the Methodist Episcopal Church was African American.[33]

History of the AME Church

Richard Allen was born a slave on February 14, 1760, in Philadelphia, Pennsylvania, and was later converted at a Methodist meeting held by a circuit rider. After his conversion he attended Methodist meetings once every two weeks. The slave owner, Stokely, was so impressed with his transformation and strong work ethic that he invited him to preach at his home. The slave master was converted and provided an opportunity for Richard and his brother to purchase their freedom for two thousand dollars in continental money.[34]

Allen taught himself to read and write and became an active member in a Delaware Methodist society in approximately 1780. He felt the call to preach the gospel of Jesus Christ and began preaching whenever and wherever he traveled in Pennsylvania and New Jersey. Allen was licensed as an exhorter in 1783. He returned to Philadelphia in 1786 and established prayer meetings for a society of forty-two African American members. He proposed a separate meeting place for the black group to worship. His idea was met with resistance, and he did not persist in starting a separate society of Methodist at that time.[35]

In April of 1787, Richard Allen and Absalom Jones organized The Free African Society in order to provide for the needs of the

---

[32] Lincoln & Mamiya, *The Black Church*, 50.

[33] Ibid.,65.

[34] Ada Strong Johnson, *History of Oak Chapel AME Church, An Historical Sketch of the Oak Chapel African Methodist Episcopal Church of Warrenton, North Carolina.* (Warrenton, NC: Jennie A. Johnson Franklin, 2007),1-2.

[35] Lincoln & Mamiya, *The Black Church*, 51.

poor. Two other purposes included racial solidarity and antislavery activities. They also met for worship services beginning in 1790. In November of 1787, Richard Allen, Absalom Jones, and another African American person arrived at St. George's Methodist Episcopal in Philadelphia and went to the altar to pray. They were pulled from the altar before they could finish their prayers, told to return to their place in the gallery. The three instead left the church, and the other black members followed them.[36]

The Free African Society took on religious activities in addition to the secular functions of the organization. From 1788 to 1791, the group that Allen called the "African Church met for worship services at the Friends Free African School House. In 1793 Richard Allen purchased land at the corner of Sixth and Lombard in the city of Philadelphia. He later moved a blacksmith shop to that corner and converted it to what would be named Bethel AME Church. This was the first black-owned church in America.[37]

The African Methodist movement spread to New Jersey, Delaware, Pennsylvania, and Maryland. In 1899 Bishop Asbury ordained Richard Allen a deacon. In 1816 five congregations joined together and formed the African Methodist Episcopal Church. At that organizational meeting, Bishop Asbury ordained Richard Allen both an itinerant elder and the first bishop of the AME Church. [38] Richard Allen remained faithful to God and the cardinal virtues of love, faith, and hope until his death in 1831. He was a committed Methodist and refused earlier opportunities to become a bishop in the African Episcopal Church. He gained the respect of many because of his commitment to order, spiritual discipline, and the simple truth of the gospel. He also organized a relief effort during the yellow fever plague, caring for the sick and burying the dead.[39]

---

36   Ibid., 50-51.

37   Ibid.,51- 52.

38   Ibid., 52.

39   Richard Allen, *The Life Experience and Gospel Labors of the Rt. Rev. Bishop Richard Allen*, (Nashville: AMEC Sunday School Union Publishing House, 1990), 1-45.

Richard Allen encouraged the AME churches to be involved in their communities by being excellent citizens. He felt that this would earn them respect from the white majority. At least three founding members of Oak Chapel were involved in the development and implementation of a volunteer black firefighters association in Warrenton, North Carolina, in 1868. They initially used oil cans for buckets to carry water from a well at the courthouse to the fire; later they used a cart or small wagon loaded with buckets and ladders. The group used oral communication to alert people of the presence of fire and designed and built wagons, shields, hooks, and chains. John S. Plummer, the great grandfather of one of the church's current members, was the first president of the black firefighters association of North Carolina. His son, who was very active in the church, has also carried on the tradition of serving the citizens of Warrenton for sixty-seven years as a volunteer firefighter, and he was president of the North Carolina Firefighters Association for three terms.[40]

The founding leaders of Oak Chapel were very industrious and served their community as a part of their faith in God. They were heavily involved in human and civil rights for oppressed people, providing a meeting place for oppressed groups of black citizens to be educated on the issues and methods to produce change in oppressive societal systems. This began in the 1860s and continues until the current time. Because the AME Church is a connectional church, the pastor has more liberty to address social and political concerns than denominations that are more locally rooted.

The African Methodist Episcopal Church has grown into an international religious organization that serves twenty Episcopal districts. The most recent addition was approximately twenty churches in India. The mission, vision, purposes, and objectives of the church were upgraded in 2008 to be more open and inclusive. There are currently over six million members of the AME Church scattered throughout the world.[41]

---

[40] Mike Legeros, *"Early Black Firefighters of North Carolina, Annotated,"* Legeros.com/history/ebf/ (Accessed January 3, 2011).

[41] *The Book of Discipline*, 2009, 1-15.

The Historic Preamble stated,

"The African Methodist Episcopal Church, whose founders affirmed their humanity in the face of slavery and racism, stands in defense of disadvantaged and oppressed peoples in the 21st century. From the origins in the Free African Society through the involvement of the AME clergy and lay in the Civil War of the 1860s and the Civil Rights Movement in the 1960s, the AMEC has preached salvation from sin and deliverance from bondage. The mission expanded to others within the African Diasporas in the Americas, Africa, Caribbean, and Europe. Whether in schools, seminaries, hospitals or social service centers, the AME Church has lived the gospel outside its sanctuaries. This mandate still informs its ministry, vision and mission in the Church's third century of existence."[42]

The mission of the AME Church is to minister to the social, spiritual, and physical development of all people. In every local church the congregation and pastor must continue to keep the vision and spirit of the Free African Society alive as they serve the needy and seek out and rescue the lost. The Church must also encourage all members to remain active in obtaining church training in all areas needed to serve God and humanity. The ultimate purposes of the AME Church are (1) make available God's biblical principles, (2) spread Christ's liberating gospel, and (3) provide continuing programs, which will enhance the entire social development of all people.[43]

The objectives of the AME Church at every level are to implement strategies to train all members in (1) Christian discipleship, (2) Christian leadership, (3) current teaching methods and materials, (4) the history and significance of the AME Church, (5) God's biblical principles, and (6) social development to which all should be applied to daily living. [44]

We teach the twenty-five Articles of Religion and the Catechism on Faith to new members so that they will understand what we believe. We live the gospel by speaking the truth in love and putting our faith into action by instilling hope in this generation. We promote

---

[42]   Ibid., 15

[43]   Ibid.

[44]   Ibid.

involvement in education, social justice, and politics to improve life and community conditions for all people.

The first Freedman School in Warrenton was operated at Oak Chapel in the 1860s. There was also a mission school held in the basement at the Warrenton Episcopal Church. Public schools for African Americans were well attended in Warrenton.[45] Two young ladies from Pennsylvania arrived in September of 1869 to teach in these schools; Margaret Newbold Thorpe and Elizabeth Pennock rented rooms from Albert Burgess and his wife, who were also political organizers for local freedmen. No hotel or boarding house would rent them rooms.[46] The African American children were very appreciative of the education provided by the two teachers.[47]

Description of Warrenton and Warren County, North Carolina

In 1860 the population of Warren country was 15,746 with 10,777 slaves, 676 free people of color, and 4,293 white people. In 1870 the population increased to 17, 768 with 12, 492 free people of color and 5, 276 white people. African Americans were able to make their voices heard because they were a majority in the county.[48] In 1870 Hyman, Cawthorne, and Falkener were re-elected to their positions in the North Carolina legislative.[49]

In 1872 Thorpe and Pennock left their teaching positions in Warrenton. [50] Hyman was re-elected to the North Carolina Senate in 1872.[51] In 1874 John Hyman was elected to the US House of

---

[45] John E. Moore, editor-in-chief, *John R. Hawkins High School Alumni Yearbook* (Warrenton, NC: John R. Hawkins Alumni and Friends, Inc.,1984), 1.

[46] Manley Wellman, *The County of Warren*, 160.

[47] Ginger Meek, *"Rich History of Church Source of Members Pride,"* 3.

[48] Wellman, *The County of Warren*, 163

[49] [49] Ibid., 165

[50] Ibid., 166.

[51] Ibid., 167.

Representatives. [52] In 1876 conservative forces mounted considerable opposition to prevent the renomination of Hyman to his former US House seat.[53] He served as a deputy collector of internal revenue for the district. Hyman left Warrenton in 1879.[54] Reverend Artts was the pastor of Oak Chapel AME Church, where John Hyman served as Sunday school superintendent until his departure and migration to Washington DC. [55] Racism was prevalent in Warren County, and many people in positions of power and influence were openly hostile toward Oak Chapel's leaders and their allies.

In the 1880s and 1890s, political power for African Americans diminished, and conservative Democrats succeeded in ousting black politicians from their positions.[56] In 1880 the Warren County census was 22,619.[57] Over the next thirty years, there was an outward migration from Warren County; in 1910 the population was 20,266.[58] In the past one hundred years the population has gone down and is estimated to be 19,425 in 2009.[59]

W. E. B. Du Bois noted the migration of blacks from the rural South to Northern cities. Between 1870 and 1970, seven million black people left the rural South to migrate to urban areas, particularly in the North, in order to escape a system of segregation and Jim Crow violence, and to obtain better jobs in order to support their families. [60] The 1890 census indicates that 90 percent of black people lived in the South with 80 percent living in the rural South. In 1980 85 percent of black people lived in urban areas.[61]

---

[52]   Ibid., 169.

[53]   Ibid., 177.

[54]   Ibid., 180-181.

[55]   Ibid., 180.

[56]   Ibid.

[57]   Ibid., 181.

[58]   Ibid., 210.

[59]   US Census Bureau, Warren County, NC, (Accessed January 3, 2011). http://quickfacts.census.gov.afd/states/37/37185.html.

[60]   Lincoln and Mamiya, *The Black Church, 118.*

[61]   Ibid., 180-181.

Oak Chapel AME Church was built to serve at least 110 parishioners. In a picture taken of the congregation around 1900, there were only five men and eighteen women, not counting the pastor.[62]The church remained with twenty-five active parishioners for the next sixty years. Urban migration took a toll on membership at the church. In the fifties and sixties, some families who were leaders in the community and church were forced out of town due to the church's involvement in the Civil Rights Movement.[63]

By 1996 the church had dwindled to nine members, and they could not continue paying the assessments of the AME Church. They wrote a letter to Bishop James and requested that the church be closed. When five members refused to sign the petition, the church remained open, but the four members who requested the church to be closed left and joined other local churches. The average age of the nine members was seventy-five.[64] Over the next nine years, the church deteriorated physically and dwindled to one active member. Several pastors of the Northern District in North Carolina tithed to the church in order to keep it open.

The one active member was transported from Fayetteville, North Carolina, to Warrenton, an approximately three-hour trip one way, once per month for a worship service in the early afternoon. In 2005 Bishop Vinton Anderson assigned a full-time student pastor to the church in order to reestablish active services for the church; that continued for two years. Locals made improvements to the building and made progress in reestablishing a small congregation. Only six of the members remained once the pastor left to start her own church in Rocky Mount, North Carolina. Of the six, only two were active attendees.

Oak Chapel was not alone as a black rural church. Lincoln and Mamiya noted that the massive migrations left a depleted population that was involved in irregular worship services and inactive ministry.[65]

---

[62]   Ginger Meek, *Warren Record*, August 1, 1990.

[63]   Catherine Smith, Oral history provided in August 2009.

[64]   Oak Chapel AME Church, Letter to the Right Bishop Frederick C. James. June 9, 1996.

[65]   Lincoln and Mamiya, *The Black Church*, 118.

They conducted a national survey of black churches in the United States over five years, beginning in 1978. They determined that the migration from 1870-1970 left rural churches with a mostly "absentee pastorate." Clergy often travelled several hundred miles to pastor a rural church, and two-thirds of the clergy lived in urban areas.[66] This has been true for Oak Chapel as well, which contributed to the church's deterioration. The last two pastors have lived closer than their predecessors; each of them lived within forty-five minutes of the church.

Poverty, Racism, and Nihilism in Warren County

Five graduate students from the School of Public Health, University of North Carolina at Chapel Hill, completed a community diagnosis of Warrenton, North Carolina, between November 2000 and March 2001. The students collected secondary data and conducted qualitative interviews of nine people, and they held five focus groups to assess community strengths and weaknesses. They identified seven areas that were perceived weaknesses of Warren County. [67] After reviewing the community diagnosis and conducting my own research, I have noted that there have not been significant changes in the past ten years.

The graduate students found that "Warren County is an economically disadvantaged area subject to both environment and social injustice."[68] They note that "old prejudices and power relationships" prevent resources from being evenly distributed to all citizens of Warren County. Even though the white citizens only represented 40 percent of the population in 2005, they held the majority of the powerful positions in the county.[69] The 2000 census in Warren County noted that the per capita income was $17,971,

---

[66]   Ibid., 95.

[67]   Carey Aselage, et al., Community Diagnosis, www.hsl.unc.edu/phpapers/warrenton/01/whistory.htm.

[68]   Ibid.

[69]   Ibid.

over $10,000 less than the state's average. The unemployment rate is one-third higher than the state average according to Employment Security Commission data in June 2006. According to the 2000 census, Warren County had a poverty rate of 19.4 percent compared to 12.3 percent for North Carolina. There is a 37 percent poverty rate for those eighteen and under.[70]The majority of jobs are low-paying service industry positions.[71] The population of Warren County has a greater percentage of elderly people than the state.[72] The group conducting the community diagnosis concludes that the area suffered from economic stagnation; there was extremely low investment in new business ventures, as well as deficient industry and business development and growth.[73] As a result of these conditions, 19 percent of the workforce of the county works outside of the county. Out of one hundred counties in North Carolina, Warren County is ninety-eighth in per capital personal income. [74]

The community members surveyed were universally concerned about the lack of retail development and the lack of opportunities to do shopping for goods and services. Community members encouraged young people to leave Warren County when they completed high school due to impoverished conditions in the area.[75] One community member stated that "for black folks, sense of community is with the church."[76]The consensus is that religion is segregated in Warren County.[77] The three major races are segregated and separated in Warren County. According to the members who participated in the study, being a newcomer decreases one's sense of community. The students conclude that community members believe that the greatest assets of Warren County are its people who volunteer in churches and

---

[70]   Ibid.
[71]   Ibid.
[72]   Ibid.
[73]   Ibid.
[74]   Ibid.
[75]   Ibid.
[76]   Ibid.
[77]   Ibid.

community organizations. Churches are the organizations that most often collaborate successfully.[78]

There are limited opportunities for recreation in Warren County. Teens at the church often complain that they are bored, because there is "nothing to do in Warren County." The educational level is lower than most other counties, and the drop-out rate is higher than most other counties. The survey concluded that the education system should be improved. Since 2001 there are now three options at the high school level. The town initiated a high-tech high school for those who are interested in technology. There is an early college option that allows students to obtain college credit while completing high school. The third is the traditional high school. The educational system has been substantially improved over the past ten years.

Warren County has no public transportation, and a significant number of people do not have access to a personal vehicle. When you walk around Warrenton, you often observe people walking or riding bikes because they do not have any other form of transportation. There are medical vans for the seniors and disabled citizens, although there is a charge for transportation to a doctor's offices or hospital in neighboring Vance County or Halifax County.

In 2009 the population estimate for Warren County was 19,425. Black person's represent53.1 percent of the population, Native Americans represent 5.1 percent of the population, white persons represent 38.5 percent, Hispanic represent 3.1 percent, and Asians represent 0.2 percent. The total non-white population is 61.5 percent of the 19,425 citizens of Warren County.[79]

The youth of Warrenton and Warren are economically disadvantaged. The local government does not provide adequate recreational programs and facilities for personal enrichment. Many families only have one parent in the home. The majority of parents are unemployed, underemployed, or working multiple low-paying jobs to provide for their families. Many communities are adversely affected by violence, addiction, and crime. Single parents often do not

---

[78] Ibid.

[79] US Census Bureau, Warren County, NC Quickfacts.census.giv/qfd/states/37/37185.html.

have adequate time to nurture their children; their long work hours contribute to a lack of guidance and supervision for the children and teens. Some youth are not encouraged to pursue higher education because of inadequate resources and a lack of hope.

Influences of Injustice on Black Youth

According to Cornel West, black working-poor communities are subjected to racial profiling, which results in grossly higher rates of conviction for illegal drug use. The prison population is disproportionately African American; there is a power imbalance between police power and the rights of poor African Americans. In this population there are visibly higher infant mortality rates, special education placements, psychic depression treatments, and unemployment levels.[80] West states, "With roughly forty percent of black children living in poverty and almost ten percent of all black young adult men in prison, we face a crisis of enormous proportions."[81] Black children are affected by historic inequalities, cultural stereotypes, double standards, and differential treatment. Living in a society that dehumanizes a person because of race ignites a deep-seated rage. Rage in the community has become the catalyst for feelings of powerlessness; poor black children are not intellectually challenged, morally empowered, or spiritually nurtured because of economic strife, social turmoil, and cultural chaos.[82] West concludes that,

> The collapse of meaning in life—the eclipse of hope and absence of love of self and others—the breakdown of family and neighborhood bonds—leads to the social deracination and cultural denouement of urban dwellers, especially children. We have created rootless, dangling people with little link to the supportive networks—family, friends, school—that sustain some sense of purpose in life. We have witnessed

---

[80]   Cornel West, *Race Matters*, XV.

[81]   Ibid., XVIII.

[82]   Ibid., 4, 8-9.

collapse of the spiritual communities that in the past helped Americans face despair, disease, and death and that transmit through the generation's dignity and decency, excellence, and elegance.[83]

People seek pleasure, power, and property in an attempt to fill the void of love, hope, and meaning. Life is difficult for the 40 percent of black children who live in poverty. These children are not equipped to live high-quality spiritual and cultural lives because of overburdened parents and bombardment with materialism by profit-hungry corporations. They need spiritual enrichment to help them counteract these conditions.

According to Cornel West, the core values advocated by black religious institutions—consisting of love, care, and service to others—have been replaced by market-driven values of pleasure, power, and acquiring possessions. Without the support and nurture available in the black church, young black people have limited means to overcome self-contempt and self-hatred perpetrated by the US capitalist society.[84] Without love, hope, and meaning, they develop nihilism, which contributes to criminal behavior.[85] West suggests that white supremacist beliefs and images that invade our culture and society contribute to emotional scars and ontological wounds that attack black character, intelligence, ability, and beauty.[86]

The founders and members of Oak Chapel AME Church experienced the effects of constant derogatory and dehumanizing words and treatment in Warren County, North Carolina. A certain person was perceived by the controlling power structures to have the political power to make positive changes for African Americans. The local newspaper demeaned and accused him of criminal and unethical conduct, which consisted of bombardment with negative and vicious attacks on his character and integrity. This eventually contributed to a violent rage against his church family. According to

---

[83]   Ibid., 9-10.

[84]   Ibid., 25-27.

[85]   Ibid., 25.

[86]   Ibid., 27.

the *Warrenton Gazette,* the renowned politician, civic and religious leader attacked his pastor twice, once in church on January 5, 1879, and again on January 6, 1879.[87] The paper never mentioned the good things that he did for the church and for the community. Some of his negative behavior could be traced to the effects of slavery and brutality that he faced over his entire life.

The history of Warren County in the 1800s totally ignores Oak Chapel AME Church except for this negative altercation. Manley Wellman discusses all the other Methodist churches that were developed during the1800s; Oak Chapel is mysteriously missing from the list as if it did not exist. The black citizens who overcame great obstacles to build a church and were pillars of the black community are also absent from the pages of the local history books. These people came together and overcame inhumanity and injustice to provide a place where black citizens could be taught, nurtured, loved, and have their hope restored. The church provided the support and guidance necessary for many to overcome evil with good. Cornel West would probably call the founders and early leaders of Oak Chapel "humble freedom fighters." [88]

The newspaper and map makers never called our church by its proper name. They called it the Colored Methodist Episcopal Church leaving out the words "Oak Chapel African" as part of its true and accurate title. The marriage bond book lists Oak Chapel as the place where many marriages took place starting in 1876. The message that sends is that the name of the church was well known but the white supremacist chose to identify it in a way that devalued us as a church.

When my family and I arrived in May of 2007, many white people of power and influence would say that they wanted to see the church restored, but they would not give any money to help the church repair the building. As we moved around in the community, they mentioned negative things that had happened in the past. One Catholic woman and a few others were an exception. Some of the local businesses would offer us a product such as a microwave, but they acted as if

---

[87]   Manley Wellman, *The County of Warren,* 180-181.
[88]   Cornel West, *Race Matters,* 31.

they could not trust the church with money. One local business was openly hostile when the church family went to buy supplies together. Attitudes of some of the white business owners in Warrenton do not seem to have changed much in the last 150 years.

Many of the black citizens that attend Oak Chapel AME Church have experienced covert and overt racism and prejudice all of their lives. The youth at the church who want to work to assist their families with their economic struggles have difficulty becoming employed in the local labor market. Cornel West states that black youth with less education and fewer opportunities suffer more from disorientation, confusion, and cultural chaos. He declared, "Ought we to be surprised that black youth are isolated from the labor market, marginalized by decrepit urban schools, devalued by alienating ideals of Afro-American beauty, and targeted by an unprecedented drug invasion, exhibit high rates of crime, and teenage pregnancy."[89] There should not be any surprise that the youth of Oak Chapel have an inner rage that contributes to self-destructive thoughts and behavior. Many of them have not grown up as regular attendees of church activities and did not get the nurture, hope, love, and meaning that only a spiritual institution can provide.

The effects of slavery have been passed to future generations. Slavery was described by W. E. B. Du Bois, as "Oppression beyond all conception: cruelty, degradation, whipping and starvation, the absolute negation of human rights . . . It was the helplessness. It was the defenselessness of family life."[90] Wimberly concludes that racism is political, structural, and symbolic. In essence he determines that black people have internalized negative stories, plots, and images as a result of being excluded from full participation in society due to being hindered from reaching their full potential.[91] He declares that

---

[89]   Ibid., 85.

[90]   Stacey Floyd- Thomas, Juan Floyd-Thomas, Carol B. Duncan, Stephen C. Ray, Jr., and Nancy Lynne Westfield, *Black Church Studies: An Introduction*, (Nashville: Abindgdon Press, 2006), 156.

[91]   Edward P. Wimberly, *African American Pastoral Care and Counseling: The Politics of Oppression and Empowerment* (Cleveland: The Pilgrim Press, 2006), 56.

fragmentation and the loss of a sense of community have caused African Americans to be disassociated and disconnected from one another in modern society.[92] Black youth and young adults who are separated from their family and communal roots become relational refugees.[93] Relationships become secondary to a virtual world constructed by a computer. The relational needs do not disappear but become subconscious. Wimberly concludes that modern addictions to food, sex, and substances become substitutes for relationships, love, and community. [94]

The youth at Oak Chapel AME Church have suffered from racism, loss of parents, poverty, and dehumanization. Many of them were isolated, marginalized, and disconnected from families and support groups prior to becoming a part of the church. When they first entered the church, they had difficulty with public speaking; they often spoke in a low voice and looked down when reading in front of the congregation. The small children would often not speak at all when they did a Sunday school lesson review in front of the congregation. Disputes, disagreements, and inappropriate language were also common during church activities.

Challenges for the Church as the Surrogate Family

The problems among black youth in Warrenton, North Carolina, are similar to what I have found in the literature, with the additional influences of rural and Southern cultures that make it a crisis of enormous proportions. I think that love—the type of love called *agape* that only God initiates—is missing. The youth need to experience the deep, Christ-centered love that transforms one's life. Many of the problems grow out of this lack of love. The anger grows to deep-seated bitterness, which progresses to various manifestations of self-hatred and hatred of others. The symptoms of this condition are rage, rebellion, disobedience, and violence. Due to the lack of loving,

---

[92]   Ibid., 20.

[93]   Ibid., 138-139.

[94]   Ibid., 139.

healing, and nurturing environments, the black youth are overexposed to the Western, individualistic, and materialistic messages that suck the life out of human beings.

The second area seems to be a lack of stable and committed relationships that honor God. The root is a basic lack of trust that originates when people in their environment are not faithful to provide the basic necessities for them to grow, develop, and thrive. The lack of faithfulness to God, one's family, the church, and the community is in need of a healing touch from Jesus. The children do not know who they can depend on when things are chaotic, confusing, and not affirming. They may feel that this poverty-stricken environment has rejected them as people, and they have difficulty making connections, communicating, and collaborating with others; this leaves them feeling isolated, lonely, and alienated.

The third area for children and youth at Oak Chapel is that they have not learned the liberating truth found in the Bible. They are missing key dietary vitamins and minerals—these deficiencies are in the spiritual diet, the intellectual diet, and the physical diet. They lack sustenance that generates life when they constantly digest destructive things in all three realms. A deficiency in truth leads to dishonesty in daily living. Self-preservation becomes important; one begins to say whatever one feels is necessary to survive for the moment. A self-centeredness that focuses on self-promotion rather than the greatest benefit for the entire community becomes a way of life. Unfortunately a self-centered mentality leads to manipulation, control, and deceit.

The fourth problem is a lack of giving. When people grow up in a poverty stricken environment, there tends to be anxiety over the resources for survival, and this sometimes leads to hoarding syndrome. There is difficulty in letting go because there is anxiety over where the resources will come from to meet tomorrow's needs. People who do not give back to God cut off their future blessings because their hands are always closed. There has been a lack of guidance from the Bible and church leaders in this area.

The fifth area of concern is unity. The emphasis in the past has been an individualistic one; this idea has been promoted by Western society. There is a belief that one cannot trust anyone else, so one must make it on one's own. There has been a loss of sense of community in the schools, churches, and other social institutions. The division between middle class and poor has grown, and society provides less contact and assistance for the disadvantaged. The poor have had the door slammed in their faces and have been treated as inferior human beings, simply because they are poor; there is little looking beyond their faults to see their needs, even in the black community. Healing needs to occur between the black middle class and the poor. Many of the churches fail to reach out to the poor—some churches leave the areas where the poor live to go to their gated communities at the lake.

Fellowship that honors Christ is lacking in our homes, churches, and communities. Nurturing takes time, but not enough time is spent with children and youth. Due to job demands, video games, and activities that foster isolation, there is a real lack of genuine fellowship. Guidance of children must be provided so that they will understand the importance of obedience to rules. Boundaries are not taught and demonstrated in our societal institutions. As a result many youths lack the firm, biblical discipline to mature and thrive in a hostile world.

There is a lack of holiness. Many churches teach the prosperity gospel and the power of positive thinking instead of righteous living.[95] There are broken relationships that have not been reconciled between God and humanity in many instances. The absence of a relationship with God leads to a lack of forgiveness between family members. Various segments of the community lack reconciliation because there has never been a genuine repentance for the dehumanization that occurred during slavery. There is a lack of trust of government and other social institutions because they have failed to meet the needs of the poor and disadvantaged and have failed to eliminate injustice, inequality, segregation, and racism in our society.

Our precious black children are stuck in a stagnant community. They reflect the failure of the church, the schools, and the community at large. They lack a structural and functional model that will improve their chances for success. The lack of love, hope, and meaning will continue to worsen unless the church develops a model that will transform their lives.

---

[95] Robert M. Franklin, *Crisis in the Village: Restoring Hope in African American Communities* (Minneapolis: Fortress Press, 2007), 112.

CHAPTER TWO

Theological Reflections of the Church as the Surrogate Family

African American youth often feel caught between two cultures and experience a duality of identity. Their African American heritage is devalued, disrespected, and demeaned by the majority in the American culture. As a result of these influences, many African American youth experience loneliness, emptiness, isolation, and alienation. They experience fragmentation, separation, and segregation in their search for genuine community. Their quest for hope, love, and meaning leads to connections with groups of their peers. Many of the negative images, stories, and identities from society become internalized. When the negative overcomes the positive, the youth attempt to fill the void more often than not with self-destructive conduct such as abuse, bullying, or violence.

The church as the surrogate family provides a solution. The family of God can become a partner with the birth family to provide a sense of belonging to African American youth. Jesus and his disciples are an example of how the church should instill hope and foster loving relationships. The family of God provides nurturing, support, and guidance through intergenerational communion and genuine fellowship. The church as the surrogate family strengthens and empowers these youth so that they are able to overcome the negative influences. African American youths are able to grow and develop healthy and strong relationships when they observe and experience genuine Christian love, loyalty, honesty, charity, fellowship, and holiness.

Theological Foundations

The church as a surrogate family is a model to address the weaknesses and lack of support voiced by African American youth. God gave humanity an instrument to transform the lives of people. What is the church? Daniel L. Migliore in *Faith Seeking Understanding* defines the church as "God's new and inclusive community of liberated creatures reconciled to God and to each other and called to God's service in the world."[96] Dietrich Bonhoeffer concludes that Jesus founded a spiritual reality that differs from the human community because it was founded on truth.[97] The local church is communal and gathers believers in Jesus Christ for loving and divine service. The church as the surrogate family is a practical theology.

We must explore what God intends for the family of God. He desires for all people to be reconciled into one spiritual family. The surrogate family does the will of God. What does the church as the surrogate family look like? How does it function to bring about spiritual formation and an interconnected community that builds loving relationships? These questions will be explored in this chapter.

Jesus did not put as much emphasis on the biological family as he did on the spiritual family. Mark writes, "Then he went home, and the crowd came together again, so that they could not even eat. When his family heard it, they went out to restrain him, for people were saying, 'He has gone out of his mind' . . . Then his mother and his brothers came; and standing outside, they sent to him and called him. A crowd was sitting around him; and they said to him, 'Your mother and your brothers and sisters are outside asking for you.' And he

---

96   Daniel L. Migliore, *Faith Seeking Understanding*, 2nd ed. (Grand Rapids: William B. Eerdman's Publishing Company, 2004), 249.

97   Dietrich Bonhoefer, *Life Together: The Classic Exploration of Christian Community. (New York: Harper & Row Publishers, Inc. 1954), 31.*

replied, 'Who are my mother, and my brothers?' And looking at those who sat around him, he said, 'Here are my mother and my brothers! Whoever does the will of God is my brother and sister and mother'" (Mark 3:18-19, 31-35).[98] This passage indicates that his disciples who do God's will are true family members.

Carolyn Osiek and David L. Balch declare that there is a contrast between the disciples who are in the house with Jesus in Mark 3:19 and his birth family who are outside the house in Mark 3:31-32.[99] The authors note that the house becomes the place of teaching rather than the synagogue as Mark's narrative develops; they see a tension between the old and the new. Osiek and Balch conclude that "since God is the only Father (Mark 11:25; 14:36; explicitly in Matt. 23:9) the patriarchal father of Mark 3: 29 is eliminated (Mark 3:30; 3:35)." The writer's observe a greater loyalty and commitment in the "new eschatological family." Jesus and the disciples have a deeper relationship based on trust and love. They note that the old household will betray the new household of Jesus (Mark 13:9-13).[100]

Lamar Williamson suggests that Mark 3:21 should be read with the Mark 3:31-35 passage in order to understand the true significance of the story.[101] "When his family heard it, they went out to restrain him, for people were saying, 'He has gone out of his mind'" (Mark 3:21). Williamson notes that the blood relatives thought Jesus was crazy; therefore they were trying to rescue him and themselves from embarrassment. There natural vision makes them blind to Jesus' true identity.[102] The disciples have had their eyes opened, and they have a spiritual vision that provides a clear image of Jesus' true identity as God's son. Their focus is on Jesus and doing the will of God even when

---

[98]   All Scriptural references are from the Holy Bible, New Revised Standard Version, (San Francisco: Harper Collins Publishers, 2007).

[99]   Carolyn Osiek and David L. Balch, Families in the New Testament World: Households and House Churches (Louisville, Westminster: John Knox Press, 1997), 127.

[100]   Ibid., 128.

[101]   Lamar Williamson, Jr., *Interpretation: A Bible Commentary for Teaching and Preaching* (Louisville: John Knox Press, 1983), 83.

[102]   Ibid., 85.

that requires that they leave behind their natural families and cling to their surrogate family.

Pheme Perkins, who wrote the commentary on the Gospel of Mark for *The New Interpreter's Bible,* said, "Jesus defines family in terms of discipleship, "those who do the will of God" (v. 35).[103] Women are present and active participants in the new family of disciples.[104] The disciples thought that Jesus' natural family was more important than they were. This passage indicates the greater importance of the surrogate family. Once a person enters the surrogate family, that person's priorities change from the natural to the spiritual, and he or she is transformed from earthly to heavenly and from temporary to permanent siblings.

When Jesus chose the first four disciples, they immediately left their fishing business and their birth family and followed him (Mark 1:16-20). Peter later questions Jesus about what their reward would be for leaving natural family and occupations behind and following him (Mark 10:28). Jesus uses the question as a teaching moment on the benefits and rewards of belonging to his true family. Jesus wants the disciples to know that their sacrifice had consequences both during their lives and for an eternity. We always seem to ask, what benefits will I receive now?

Jesus states, "Truly I tell you, there is no one who has left house or brothers or sisters or mother or father or children or fields, for my sake and for the sake of the good news, who will not receive a hundredfold now in this age—houses, brothers and sisters, mothers and children, and fields with persecutions—and in the age to come eternal life" (Mark 10:29-30).

Jesus instructs the disciples on their relationship with God and with one another in the family of God. He distinguishes between the scribes and the Pharisees and them. In the family of God there must be humility; arrogance and pride have no place in His household. Spiritual formation and redemption reverses the script in our hearts

---

[103] Pheme Perkins, "The Gospel of Mark: Introduction, Commentary, and Reflections," *The New Interpreter's Bible,* vol. 8, (Nashville: Abingdon Press, 1994), 566.

[104] Ibid., 567.

and minds. Love replaces hate. Communion and fellowship replace individuality. Our own desires are replaced by what is best for all in the village. Who is the one who unites us for a greater good for all to experience?

Jesus explains, "But you are not to be called rabbi, for you have one teacher, and you are all students, and call no one your father on earth, for you have one Father—the one in heaven. Nor are you to be called instructors, for you have one instructor, the Messiah. The greatest among you will be your servant. All who exalt themselves will be humbled, and all who humble themselves will be exalted" (Matt. 23:8-12).

Osiek and Bolch define family as a kinship group in the traditional Mediterranean society, which is "a diachronic and synchronic association of persons related by blood or marriage, and other social conventions, organized for the dual purpose of enhancement of its social status and legitimate transfer of property."[105] These authors state that there was no direct translation from Greek, Hebrew, or Latin to modern Western English for "family" or "house."[106] The church as the surrogate family would fit the traditional definition of family with some adaptations. The intentional gathering of persons that become a spiritual group for the purpose of spiritual formation and growth of all and who will all inherit a spiritual kingdom could be one definition of the surrogate family. The origin of the family is spiritual, but it produces healthy people within the family in all realms of life from the inner spirit to the outer physical body.

Osiek and Balch note that commitment to Jesus is primary.[107] A primary allegiance to Jesus is evident in his statement: "Follow me, and let the dead bury their own dead" (Matt. 8:22). The spiritually alive must continue to be committed to enlarging the family of God. The spiritually dead can bury the physically dead. The disciples have a higher mission to proclaim the word of God that restores abundant life. The authors provide a second example of the "ultimate

---

[105] Osiek and Blach, *Families in the New Testament World, 41.*

[106] Ibid., 6.

[107] Ibid., 131.

commitment to Jesus" in Matthew 10: 34-39.[108] Jesus tells the disciples that they must give up their whole life in order to experience the true life, stating, "Those who find their life will lose it, and those who lose their life for my sake will find it" (Matt. 10:39). How did the concept of the spiritual family evolve into what we know as the local church?

Osiek and Balch discover a major advantage for "use of the family as a model for the church," concluding that the church as the surrogate family promotes an inclusive open house environment where all could learn in relationship to Jesus and one another. They saw how Jesus brought people that were different together in order to pursue the mission of building the kingdom of God.[109] Osiek and Balch observe that in the family there is respect, obedience, and a duty to provide for the needy, especially the widows and orphans.[110] Matthew writes that tax collectors and prostitutes were warmly welcomed into the new family (Matt. 21:28-32).[111] The strength of the community was based on genuine love that embraced diversity. Those at the margins brought support to one another, so that no one lacked anything they needed.

Joseph H. Hellerman articulates the theology of the church as the surrogate family better than any other theologian of the twenty-first century. He indicates that much of American evangelical theology emphasizes the manger and the cross. The majority of these theologians provide a superficial coverage of the life of Jesus between his birth and resurrection. Hellerman calls the church back to recover "Jesus' vision for authentic Christian community" through an in-depth analysis of orthopraxis. He challenges the Christian community to examine the interpersonal relationships of Jesus and his disciples.[112]

Hellerman declares, "The time has come for us to pursue a more holistic and biblical Christology, one which unites belief and

---

[108]   Ibid.

[109]   Ibid., 221.

[110]   Ibid., 166.

[111]   Ibid., 133.

[112]   Joseph H. Hellerman, *When the Church Was a Family: Recapturing Jesus' Vision for Authentic Christian Community* (Nashville: B & H Publishing Group, 2009), 62.

behavior in a way that is consistent with the teachings and practice of New Testament Christianity." According to Hellerman, this is what orthopraxis, "right behavior," is all about. "We are now prepared to consider orthopraxis, as Jesus understood it, with respect to two important institutions in the ancient world—the natural family and the surrogate family of God that Jesus was gathering around Him during His earthly ministry."[113] When we contrast the two, we are able to catch Jesus' vision.

Hellerman calls Jesus and his disciples a surrogate family. [114] Hesuggests that Jesus intentionally chose the term "family" as a social metaphor to describe his community.[115] There is an equality, mutuality, and inclusiveness in this new spiritual surrogate family that supersedes the biological family. Jesus interconnects the new family together in such a way that they are constantly being built up and encouraged. In community they experience a sense of belonging; they receive support and guidance to achieve their purpose. Collectively they are enhanced to go beyond their wildest imagination. What type of clinical education does Jesus provide for the disciples, and how can we replicate the process?

Jesus provides on-the-job training for his disciples, as well as a model of nurturing that is second to none. First they were built up by his love and presence as he taught them key biblical principles. Each miracle was a teaching moment so that they could grow in trust, faith, and commitment. As they grew in relationship to him and one another, he expanded their world. He never wasted a teaching moment on his journey through practical ministry. They observed powerful healings, deliverances, and resurrections from the dead. After observing many different miracles, they were empowered to be instruments of his will to bring health and wholeness to a desperate and dying world. How did Paul build on the foundation that Jesus laid?

---

[113] Joseph H. Hellerman, *When the Church Was a Family: Recapturing Jesus' Vision for Authentic Christian Community* (Nashville: B & H Publishing Group, 2009), 62.

[114] Ibid., 64.

[115] Joseph H. Hellerman, *Jesus and the People of God: Reconfiguring Ethnic Identity.* (Sheffield: Phoenix Press, 2007), 286.

Robert J. Banks documents the family metaphor as the most common term used for the Christian community in Pauline writings.[116] He determines that Paul portrayed the Christian community as a divine, living family that grows to maturity through interdependence.[117] We note that Paul usually begins and ends each book that he wrote with a greeting to his brothers. "I commend to you our sister Phoebe . . . welcome her in the Lord as is fitting for the saints, and help her in whatever she may require from you, for she has been a benefactor of many and of myself as well" (Rom. 16:1-2).

Paul explains how all God's people, both Jews and Gentiles, came to be one family. Abraham and his descendants received their inheritance through the righteousness of faith (Rom. 4:13). Paul declares, "For this reason it depends on faith, in order that the promise may rest on grace and be guaranteed to all his descendants, not only to the adherents of the law but also to those who share the faith of Abraham (for he is the father of all of us, as it is written, 'I have made you the father of many nations')—in the presence of the God in whom he believed, who gives life to the dead and calls into existence the things that do not exist. Hoping against hope, he believed that he would become the father of many nations," according to what was said: "So numerous shall your descendants be" (Rom. 4: 16-18).

Paul teaches how we become children of God and what it means to be a child of God. He says, "For all who are led by the Spirit of God are children of God," (Rom. 8:14) and explains, "When we cry, 'Abba! Father!' it is that very Spirit bearing witness with our spirit that we are children of God, and if children, then heirs, heirs of God and joint heirs with Christ—if, in fact we suffer with him so that we may also be glorified with him" (Rom. 8:15-17). There is freedom from decay for the children of God (Rom. 8:21). Jesus is "the firstborn within a large family" (Rom. 8:29). Paul discusses how the family of God is strengthened and how we are conformed to the image of Jesus the Christ. He states, "Likewise the Spirit helps us in our weakness; for we

---

[116] Robert J. Banks, *Paul's Idea of Community: The Early House Churches in Their Cultural Setting*, rev. ed. (Peabody, MA: Hendrickson Publishers, Inc. 1994), 49.

[117] Ibid., 47, 49.

do not know how to pray as we ought, but that very Spirit intercedes with sighs too deep for words. And God, who searches the heart, knows what is the mind of the Spirit, because the Spirit intercedes for the saints according to the will of God" (Rom. 8:26-27).

In the family of God there is equality. In our world we experience inequality through racism, sexism, and classism. God's family does not distinguish between the rich and the poor; there is mutual love and respect among family members. The distinctions that cause division, separation, and segregation are eliminated in God's family. Paul concluded, "For in Christ Jesus you are all children of God through faith. As many of you as were baptized into Christ have clothed yourself with Christ. There is no longer Jew or Greek, there is no longer slave or free, there is no longer male and female; for all of you are one in Christ Jesus. And if you belong to Christ, then you are Abraham's offspring, heirs according to the promise" (Gal. 3:26-29). The church as the surrogate family challenges the modern and often unbalanced view of family.

Paul speaks of his relationship with the church at Thessalonica in kinship terms. He provides an example for any pastor regarding how she should provide pastoral care to the local church family. He uses terms that demonstrate his love and compassion for them. Paul establishes a standard for future pastors. The standard has not changed since the beginning of the church, though there are of course different cultural expressions of pastoral care.

> But we were gentle among you, like a nurse tenderly caring for her own children. So deeply do we care for you that we are determined to share with you not only the gospel of God but also our own selves, because you have become very dear to us. You remember our labor and toil, brothers and sisters; we worked night and day, so that we might not burden any of you while we proclaimed to you the gospel of God. You are witnesses, and God also, how pure, upright, and blameless our conduct was toward you believers. As you know, we dealt with each one of you like a father with his children, urging and encouraging you and pleading that you lead a life worthy of God, who calls you into his own kingdom and glory (1 Thess. 2:7b-12).

Paul also commands, "Do not speak harshly to an older man, but speak to him as to a father, to younger men as brothers, to older women as mothers, to younger women as sisters—with absolute purity" (1 Tim. 5:1). Older women are to teach, encourage, and nurture the younger women in the church (Titus 2:3-4). Paul refers to Timothy as "my child" (2 Tim. 2:1) and demonstrates that the divine family is blessed and enlightened by "the God of our Lord Jesus Christ, the Father of glory" (Eph. 1:17). His frequent use of kinship terms provides a model for the church as the surrogate family to follow. How has the church furthered the model developed by Jesus and expanded by Paul?

Miguel A. De La Torre describes the church as a family because it can never be confined to a building.[118] The church as the surrogate family is a supernatural organism that was created by God. There are no limits to what God can do through his divine creation. The church is similar to the glorified body that all members will have in heaven. The church body moves about throughout the world to build up and enlarge the family. The church shall prevail because it is the embodied presence of the living God. There are no boundaries other than the ones set by God. All creations of humanity have limits, but God created the church to be without limits. What does a church as the surrogate family look like without walls?

The family of God promotes justice and confronts evil everywhere and all the time. Emerson Powery declares, "For Jesus, family is anyone who stays in the struggle, anyone who does 'the will of God,' who continues to fight against the dehumanizing forces of evil, who engages head-on the societal institutional structures of deprivation that keeps humans down."[119] The love of Jesus produces spiritual and social solidarity that calls for his disciples to stand with the oppressed and against the oppressors. The family of Jesus spoke out against evil

---

118 Miguel A. De La Torre, "Pastoral Care from the Latina/o Margins," eds. Sheryl A. Kujawa Holbrook and Karen B. Montagno, *Injustice and the Care of Souls* (Minneapolis: Fortress Press, 2009), 69.

119 Emerson B. Powery, "The Gospel of Mark," ed. Brian K. Blount, *True to Our Native Land: An African American New Testament Commentary* (Minneapolis: Fortress Press, 2007), 128.

structures and systems that failed to follow God's will. The church as the surrogate family must promote social justice and foster true freedom throughout the world.

The *Africa Bible Commentary* notes that Jesus demonstrated that the true test of kinship is spiritual rather than natural.[120] A person must be born into the family of God in order to do the will of God (John 1:12-13). Jesus said, "Very truly, I tell you, no one can enter the kingdom of God without being born of water and Spirit. What is born of flesh is flesh, and what is born of the Spirit is spirit. Do not be astonished that I said to you, 'You must be born from above'" (John 3:5-7).

When we are born from above, we surrender our will to struggle for self-fulfillment. Our will becomes one with the will of God when we are enlightened by the grace and truth of Jesus Christ. This transformation comes when we step out of our will and into the will of God. When we are obedient to the will of God, we gain the blessings and favor of God. We become one with Jesus when we yield control to him through the Holy Spirit and conduct ourselves as Jesus did during his three years of earthly ministry. Our behavior changes from self-centered to Christ-centered because of the influence of the fruit of the Spirit.

The contrast between the surrogate family and the natural family helps distinguish between the will of God and the natural will of individual human beings. The natural will is inwardly focused; the will of God is outwardly focused. Jesus was active in restoring what was lost. He restored physical health to those who were suffering from various diseases and injuries. He restored freedom to those who were held captive by oppressive institutions and governments. He restored life to the dead. Jesus delivered those being oppressed by demonic forces so their mental faculties could be restored.

---

[120] Victor Babaajide Cole, "Mark," ed. Tokunboh Adeyemo, *Africa Bible Commentary: A One-Volume Commentary.* (New York: The Zondervan Corporation, 2006), 1178.

Theological Reflections of the Black Church as Surrogate Family

Jesus demonstrated the will of God so people would have a model for Christians to follow. Shawn Copeland has identified four practical principles in black theology that follows the mission and ministry of Jesus. She notes that black theology must speak divine truth to the chaos and confusion of "imperial globalization." Copeland states, "This theology must provide practical solutions to the suffering of poor African Americans that will provide relief to them. According to Copeland, Black theology must resist evil in creative and practical ways. She states that the orthopraxis of black theology instills hope through creating healthy holistic communities."[121]

Emmanuel Y. Lartey defines pastoral theology as the interconnection of faith and practice.[122] He suggests that "God is communal."[123] Lartey says, "The church as a relational and corporate community is both the base and agent of care.[124] Lartey states, "Communities of faith are the loci of pastoral care and pastoral theology properly understood and practiced."[125] The church as the surrogate family is the practical application of pastoral theology. Lartey concludes that the primary task of pastoral theology is to facilitate the development of hope, love, and meaning in a community that respects individuality but encourages healthy holistic relationships.[126] He quotes Cornel West, who in *Race Matters* wrote a description of nihilism that must be overcome in the African American community.[127]

---

[121] M. Shawn Copeland, "Living Stones in the Household of God," ed. Linda E. Thomas, *Living Stones in the Household of God: The Legacy and Future of Black Theology* (Minneapolis: Fortress Press, 2004), 188.

[122] Emmanuel Y. Lartey, *Pastoral Theology in an Intercultural World.* (Cleveland: The Pilgrim Press, 2006), 121.

[123] Ibid., 119.

[124] Ibid., 123.

[125] Ibid.

[126] Ibid., 143.

[127] Ibid.

> Nihilism is to be understood here not as a philosophic doctrine that there are no rational grounds for legitimate standards or authority; it is, far more, the lived experience of coping with a life of horrifying meaninglessness, hopelessness, and (most important) love-lessness. The frightening result is a numbing detachment from others and a self-destructive disposition toward the world. Life without meaning, hope, and love breeds a coldhearted, mean-spirited outlook that destroys both the individual and others. [128]

Edward and Anne Wimberly and Anne Grace Chingonzo conclude that African American churches must restore village functions by implementing a model that provides care and nurture.[129] They describe a mini village model that empowers and mentors children and youth through cross-generational worship, Bible study, and teaching and learning. "Large congregations implement the class meeting model that provides an opportunity for fellowship, care, encouragement, and nurture in addition to the traditional weekly services of preaching and teaching.[130]"The authors conclude that, "Human connectedness beyond the nuclear family is essential for human beings to flourish. People need the semblance of the small village and its functions to survive. The local congregation will be one important venue for restoring village functions, and pastoral care and counseling will play a significant role in the restoration of the village functions." [131]

Lonzy F. Edwards, Sr., who is an attorney and pastor, suggests that pastoral theology should be holistic, provide social action to address social and economic oppression, and shepherd the larger

---

[128] Cornel West, *Race Matters* (New York: Vintage Books, 19947), 22-23

[129] Edward Wimberly, Annie Streaty Wimberly, and Annie Grace Chingonzo, "Pastoral Counseling, Spirituality and the Recovery of the Village Functions: African and Africa-American Correlates in the Practice of Pastoral Care and Counseling," eds. John Foskett and Emmanuel Lartey, *Spirituality and Culture in Pastoral Care and Counseling: Voices from Different Contexts* (Fairwater, Cardiff: Cardiff Academic Press, 2004), 30.

[130] Ibid., 24.

[131] Ibid., 30.

community.[132] Ministry in the African American church must seek to transform the community.[133] The church must provide a prophetic voice to society that advocates for social justice and challenges stagnant social systems.[134] The surrogate family does the will of God by speaking the truth to the power structures of society. The collective voice of a well-organized congregation can be an ambassador for change within the larger community. Jesus challenges the societal and religious power structures, confronting the leaders of the institutions that relied on the law rather than on God.

In *Meet Me at the Palaver,* Tapiwa N. Mucherera provides a model for restoring hope to orphans and widows in Zimbabwe, Africa. "Even though many of their natural families have been destroyed by HIV, war, and famine as a result of severe poverty there is still 'hope in God and in the family of God found in community.'"[135] Mercy Oduyoye, a Nigerian theologian, indicates that one's sense of self-identity derives from their relationship with God, other humans, and creation.[136] Mucherera concludes that the global village needs a communitarian theology that knows no national boundaries.[137] A crisis anywhere in the world will impact all other areas sooner or later; therefore we must be concerned about our neighbor and the survival of humanity now.[138] According to Mucherera, religion is the first theological signpost of hope.[139]

Mucherera proposes a model that utilizes the church as the best place to implement revillaging similar to the palaver setting in

---

132 Lonzy F. Edwards, Sr., *Pastoral Care of the Oppressed: A Reappraisal of the Social Crisis Ministry of African-American Churches. (Macon, GA: Magnolia Publishing Company, 1997),* 208.

133 Ibid., 209.

134 Ibid., 210.

135 Tapiwa N. Mucherera, *Meet Me at the Palaver: Narrative Pastoral Counseling in Postcolonial Contexts* (Eugene, OR: Cascade Books, 2009), 134.

136 Ibid., 83.

137 Ibid., 84.

138 Ibid., 84,88.

139 Ibid., 76.

Zimbabwe.[140] Revillaging is the second theological signpost of hope.
[141]The concept of reclaiming the traditional core values of Africa is
revillaging.[142] All humans are interconnected and interdependent.[143]
Hope is instilled in younger and future generations through mentoring
relationships.[144]

Mucherera suggests reauthoring the stories by challenging selfish,
greedy, corrupt, and oppressive postcolonial governments who create
economic crises.[145] Reauthoring is the third signpost of hope.[146] He
describes reauthoring as the weaving together of hopeful biblical
stories with one's own stories to create "a new and hopeful story."
[147]Reauthoring helps the indigenous peoples overcome the inferiority
complex imposed on them by Western society.[148] Once the reauthoring
process is initiated, people begin to think and talk more positively
about themselves.

Mucherera states, "In the African context, one's life and stories
unfold within the context of community, and this is therefore
acknowledged that it is within community relations that health can
be achieved."[149] Healthy interdependence is the goal for all people of
all ages.[150] He advocates a holistic counseling method that provides
health and healing for the body, mind, and spirit.[151] The pastoral
counselor must first attend to the physical needs by connecting the
person with someone who can service their physical needs.[152]

---

[140] Ibid.,89.

[141] Ibid., 76.

[142] Ibid., 89.

[143] Ibid., 97.

[144] Ibid.

[145] Ibid.

[146] Ibid.,76.

[147] Ibid., 95.

[148] Ibid.

[149] Ibid., 101.

[150] Ibid., 102.

[151] Ibid., 102-103.

[152] Ibid., 103.

James writes,

> What good is it, my brothers and sisters, if you say you have faith but do not have works? Can faith save you? If a brother or sister is naked and lacks daily food, and one of you says to them, "Go in peace, keep warm and eat your fill," and yet you do not supply their basic needs, what is the good of that? So faith by itself, if it has no works, is dead . . . For just as the body, without the spirit is dead, so faith without works is also dead. (James 2:14-17).

Mucherera declares that the second priority in the holistic approach is caring for the emotional and psychological needs of the person.[153] The church as the surrogate family provides an opportunity for children and youth to share their concerns with others; they learn that their voice matters and they will be heard. Dialogue helps facilitate the recovery process. Past abuse and trauma must be openly discussed with caring and empathetic counselors before healing can begin. Pastors who are properly educated can provide and facilitate the healing process. This can be accomplished in a loving, supportive, and nurturing community such as a local congregation.

The third priority according to Mucherera is to provide the resources for meeting spiritual needs.[154] People need to understand where God is in their crises.[155] God is always with them and will never forsake them because he is omnipresent. Jesus is the healer who understands their grief and loss. Many times people need compassionate, pastoral care in order to understand where God is in their crises.

Jesus was concerned about the whole person. He had compassion for those who were suffering due to physical, psychological, and spiritual problems. Over five thousand people went three days without food while they listened to his sermons in a remote area. He borrowed a boy's lunch and prayed for God to bless the five barley loaves and two small fish. As a result of his compassion, no one went hungry.

---

[153]   Ibid.

[154]   Ibid.

[155]   Ibid.,104.

Jesus healed the sick and cast out demons on a regular basis during his three-year ministry. Jesus always dealt with their most serious problem first, and most of the miracles concerned physical healing. As a result of him meeting their physical needs, they believed and were saved.

Jesus healed the man born blind before he revealed himself as the Son of God (John 9:7-8; 35-38). The woman caught in the act of adultery was creatively protected from stoning (John 8:3-9). Jesus pronounced forgiveness and said, "Go your way and from now on do not sin again (John 8:10-11). Jesus demonstrated the power of God's love. As practical theologians we, too, must have an incarnational ministry.

Tapiwa Mucherera describes the concept of utilizing the palaver "to resolve a problem, crisis, or conflict and to make other time for educational purposes or just simply for fellowship."[156] He notes that Robert G. Armstrong translated the word palaver into the phrase, "the public meeting."[157] Armstrong defines palaver as "any gathering of an organized group in a formal manner." [158] According to Mucherera, a palaver is a traditional African means of processing disputes and promoting healing for individuals and communities. [159]

In the African model palaver, an elder of the community listens to the struggles and the painful encounters of the day or another brief period of time.[160] According to Mucherera, "The community elder tells stories that promote encouragement and wisdom. The African community palaver usually occurs in the evening or night. The participants sit in a circle under a tree or around a fire." The village meetings have been effective in providing wisdom and guidance for orphaned children and widows so that they are able to process their losses and make plans for the future. [161]

---

156   Ibid.,109.
157   Ibid.
158   Ibid.
159   Ibid.
160   Ibid.
161   Ibid.,110.

The church palaver provides spiritual support through fellowship, prayer, and worship. The leader who facilitates the discussion makes sure that everyone has an opportunity to share, contribute, and ask questions.[162] "Any problem that is discussed is shared by all in the circle. The elder emphasizes that the problem is external to the identity of the person. The person with the issue is not the problem. The church palaver seeks to restore hope through a series of questions and the reauthoring process."[163]

At the palaver Mucherera notes that orphaned children and widows could talk about sex and death.[164] Traditional church groups have not openly discussed these issues. The problem loses its power when the truth is spoken in love within a supportive, caring, and nurturing community.[165] The palaver offers eternal hope through the love, education, and liberating truth in Jesus the Christ.[166] Mucherera provides several examples of how the church palaver empowered and encouraged orphans to thrive and care for their younger siblings without having to be placed in an orphanage.[167] The facilitation of honest conversation occurs in genuine community.

C. Anthony Hunt suggests that ministry to the poor should reflect a "reaching and looking across" rather than a top-down approach. He advocates empowerment and long range solutions rather than short-term Band-Aids. Hunt focuses on ministry to the poor that provides liberation through justice, economic growth, and self-reliance.[168] "As new people are integrated into the church, they must 'become active and contributing participants in Christ's ministry.'"[169] Hunt concludes that the church must avoid a complete vertical ministry to their

---

[162] Ibid.

[163] Ibid., 111,113.

[164] Ibid.,126.

[165] Ibid.

[166] Ibid.

[167] Ibid.

[168] C. Anthony Hunt, *The Black Family: The Church Role in the African American Community.* (Bristol, IN: Wyndham Hall Press, 2000), 23.

[169] Ibid., 39.

needs, but seek to minister *with* them to others.[170] He suggests that churches should be in solidarity with the poor.[171]

In *Race, Racism, and Reconciliation* Gilbert Caldwell writes, "We believe God is creator and parent. God is an equal opportunity creator and parent. We are not created by God to be rich or poor, powerful or powerless. We of the church believe that every creature on the earth was created by God and we thus share the same parent, and we are brothers and sisters. We must see to it that our brothers and sisters do not suffer."[172] When they suffer, we must suffer. Hunt discovers that the black church offers hope through their sermons and songs that promote recovery from addiction. He also notes that those who struggle are seeking ministry that puts the church's words into action.[173] Practical ministry is desperately needed to empower and liberate the body, mind, and spirit from oppression.

In *Soul Theology*, Nicholas Cooper-Lewter and Henry Mitchell affirm the biblical principle that all humanity is related as a family.[174] They suggest that the Church as the family of God is "seriously practiced" in the black church even though it is not discussed in theory.[175] Their belief that all humanity belongs to one kinship group influences their interaction in the traditional Black community. "The title for men and women in the church and in the street are brother and sister."[176] Cooper-Lewter and Mitchell note that growing up in a loving family fosters a healthy sense of uniqueness and equality, which is critical for endurance and survival in an oppressive sociopolitical environment.[177]

A Yoruba proverb states, "He who has the support of others can achieve great things."[178] According to Cooper-Lewter and Mitchell,

---

170 Ibid.

171 Ibid., 23.

172 Ibid., 33.

173 Ibid., 29.

174 Nicholas Cooper- Leweter and Henry H. Mitchell, *Soul Theology: The Heart of American Black Culture* (Nashville: Abingdon Press, 1991), 127.

175 Ibid.

176 Ibid., 128.

177 Ibid., 128.

178 Ibid., 129.

the communal support that developed during slavery assisted the extended families with enduring extensive and brutal hardships. "People who belong to an oppressed group need close family interaction, unconditional acceptance, and serious mutual obligation in order to survive and thrive."[179] An undying love and commitment to one another instills hope. Jesus modeled the unconditional love and compassion for his disciples, and the disciples continued this pattern of initiating churches throughout the world. Even though many have tried to destroy the church, the unconditional love, acceptance, hope, and sense of purpose has empowered it to persevere. The surrogate family that Jesus developed with his group of disciples must be replicated in order for the current generation to overcome hostilities against the church.

Love is not something that can be easily defined. Love is experienced through a community that provides meaning and instills hope. Genuine love is an active partnership between God and his family. In their book *Balm in Gilead*, Toinette M. Eugene and James Newton Poling determine that the relationship between love and justice is practiced through the priestly ministry and the prophetic ministry of the black church. They suggest that priestly ministry provides the love manifested in healing, comforting, and succoring work. The prophetic ministry provides teaching, preaching, and social justice that transforms the families and communities. They conclude that the two ministries together end abuse and violence that cause injury to the spirit, mind, and body.[180]

In *Redemption in Black Theology,* Olin Moyd proclaims that the black church was the redemptive center that provided meaning and stability for black people gathered together in the church setting.[181] Eugene and Poling identify the black church as the extended family that nurtures the African American community. They view the black

---

[179]   Ibid., 132.

[180]   Toinette M. Eugene and James Newton Poling, *Balm for Gilead: Pastoral Care for African American Families Experiencing Abuse* (Nashville: Abingdon Press, 1998), 21-22. Eugene and Poling, *Balm for Gilead*, 28.

[181]   Olin Moyd, *Redemption in Black Theology* (Valley Forge, PA: Judson Press, 1979), 199.

church as an organism that takes the broken pieces and remolds them into a wonderful new creation by enhancing greater love, faith, trust, and shared values.[182] Eugene and Poling conclude that God provides the power for renewal and the discovery of a deeper identity as a "Balm in Gilead."[183]

Jesus the healer works through the black church to restore and revitalize the soul of the community participants. The churches that function as surrogate families are community healers. Family members enter into solidarity with people who have experienced abuse and violence; when the scars are deep, they must be recovered in order to become healed. The black church provides a forum for expression and processing painful experiences in a loving, nurturing, and supportive community. Many forms of artistic expression are employed to facilitate the transformation from broken to whole. Music, dance, and biblical drama provide an avenue for artistic expression, which fosters healing.

The black church provides practical education in a supportive environment. Much emphasis is placed on the application of what they have learned from biblical principles. Youth experience an open and interactive dialogue that fosters personal and spiritual growth and development. The church as the surrogate family is essential to this process.

Yolanda Y. Smith, in her chapter from the book *In Search of Wisdom*, states, "That all models of sharing wisdom in the black church with children and youth must embrace their triple heritage. The three components of that heritage which must be included are: Christian roots, African culture, and black American identity." [184] According to Anne Wimberly and Evelyn Parker, black churches are "essential faith 'villages' that generate wisdom through the sharing of

---

182 Eugene and Poling, *Balm for Gilead*, 28.

183 Ibid., 34.

184 Yolanda Y. Smith, "Forming Wisdom through Cultural Rootedness," eds. Anne E. Streaty Wimberly and Evelyn Parker, *In Search of Wisdom: Faith Formation in the Black Church* (Nashville: Abingdon Press, 2002), 43.

gifts of inspiration, information, encouragement, time, and praise."[185] The holistic approach makes sure that every aspect of their being is embraced; they learn to feel good about themselves as a member of God's surrogate family.

There is a relationship between Jesus and his disciples that takes priority over the biological family. The concept that brings the spiritual family together is doing the will of God. How does Jesus define the will of God? In Matthew 25 Jesus describes those who would inherit the kingdom of God: "for I was hungry and you gave me food, I was thirsty and you gave me something to drink, I was a stranger and you welcomed me, I was naked and you gave me clothing, I was sick and you took care of me, I was in prison and you visited me" (Matt. 25:35-36).

The people who thought that they were righteous asked when Jesus had experienced hunger, thirst, nakedness, and imprisonment, and had been a stranger. Jesus refers to his spiritual family as having equality with him when he says, "And the king will answer them, 'Truly I tell you, just as you did it to one of the least of these who are members of my family, you did it to me' (Matt. 25: 37-40). The disciples who were standing around while Jesus was teaching believed and accepted him as Lord and Savior. They followed him and performed ministry to the sick and disabled. They preached repentance and gathered people into the family of God.

As family members, the disciples took responsibility for one another; they were involved in building up one another and in building God's kingdom. These disciples who followed Jesus were ordinary women and men who loved God and had compassion for those who suffered from various afflictions. They had placed their faith in Jesus and trusted God. Like Jesus they left behind biological families and possessions to do God's will exclusively. Jesus commanded, "But strive first for the kingdom of God and his righteousness, and all these things will be given to you as well" (Matt. 6:33).

---

[185] Anne E. Streaty Wimberly and Evelyn L. Parker, *In Search of Wisdom: Faith Formation in the Black Church* (Nashville, Abingdon Press, 2002), 17.

Theological Reflections on Surrogate Family Themes

The leading factor that distinguishes a member of the family of God is love. John writes, "See what love the Father has given us that we should be called the children of God; and that is what we are. The reason the world does not know us is that it did not know him. Beloved, we are God's children now; what we will be has not yet been revealed. What we do know is this: when he is revealed, we will be like him, for we will see him as he is" (1 John 3:1-2). Love prevents us from hating our enemies. Jesus calls us to love and pray for our enemies and forgive those who have sinned against us (Luke 6:27-28, 37).

People need and desire love. The mutuality of giving and receiving love is important to achieving health and wholeness. Jesus explains to the disciples, "As the Father has loved me, so I have loved you; abide in my love. If you keep my commandments, you will abide in my love, just as I have kept my Father's commandments and abide in his love . . . This is my commandment, that you love one another as I have loved you" (John 15:9-10, 12). The greatest power on earth is love. The family of God can overcome all things through the sharing of God's love. The power of God's love defeats evil. There are no boundaries to the sacrificial love of Jesus the Christ. How does love become manifested in a transformative community?

Martin Luther King, Jr. writes much about the power of love. He used the Greek word *agape,* which the Bible uses to explain the orthopraxis of God's love. We will see in this revelation what Jesus really meant when he said that we should love God and our neighbor. We come to understand the power of God's love when we experience the liberating and redemptive power of the cross of Jesus. King's definition of *agape* demonstrates how shackles are broken and enemies become friends.

> *Agape* means understanding, redeeming good will for all men. It is an overflowing love which is purely spontaneous, unmotivated, groundless, and creative. It is not set in motion by any quality or function of its object. It is the love of God operating in the human heart.

> *Agape* is disinterested love. It is a love in which the individual seeks not his own good, but the good of his neighbor. (Cor. 10:24)
>
> Another basic point about *agape* is that it springs from the *need* of the other person—his need for belonging to the best in the human family.
>
> *Agape* is not a weak, passive love. It is love in action. Agape is love seeking to preserve and create community. It is insistence on community even when one seeks to break it. *Agape* is a willingness to go to any length to restore community. It doesn't stop at the first mile, but it goes the second mile to restore community. It is a willingness to forgive, not seven times, but seventy times seven to restore community. The cross is the eternal expression of the length to which God will go in order to restore broken community. The resurrection is a symbol of God's triumph over all the forces that seek to block community. The Holy Spirit is the continuing community creating reality that moves through history.[186]

The family of God is characterized by loyalty. Paul declares, "God is faithful; by him you were called into the fellowship of his Son, Jesus Christ our Lord" (1 Cor. 1:9). John called Jesus, the rider on the white horse, "Faithful and True" (Rev. 19:11). David states, "Love the Lord, all you his saints. The Lord preserves the faithful" (Ps. 31:23). Jesus tells a parable to distinguish between the faithful servant and the wicked and lazy servant. Of the faithful servant he says, "Well done, good and trustworthy slave; you have been trustworthy in a few things, so I will put you in charge of many things; enter into the joy of your master" (Matt. 25:23).

Paul lists faithfulness as one of the nine fruit of the spirit (Gal. 5:22). Spiritual family members are loyal to one another; they provide support both in good times and in times of challenge and crisis. A member of God's family is never forsaken. The presence of the Holy

---

[186] James M. Washington, ed., *A Testament of Hope: The Essential Writings and Speeches of Martin Luther King, Jr.* (New York: Harper Collins, 1986), 19-20.

Spirit provides comfort and guidance. The hand of God directs other family members to show compassion in times of need. The spiritual family should be dependable and reliable. We should be able to trust them to do the will of God and continue to build God's kingdom. When a particular spiritual family fails to provide compassionate and nurturing care, God will provide some alternative to facilitate healing.

Honesty and truthfulness are discovered in God's family. Jesus states, "These are the ones who, when they hear the word, hold it fast in an honest and good heart, and bear fruit with patient endurance" (Luke 8:15). Truth is valued in God's family. People are more likely to hear the truth when they discuss their issues with other spiritual family members. The truth can sometimes be hidden in our subconscious. The Holy Spirit will eventually uncover information that leads to an understanding of relevant truth. Many times God uses others in the family of God in this process.

Jesus said to Thomas, "I am the way, and the truth, and the life; No one comes to the Father except through me" (John 14: 6). Jesus explains to the disciples that they will receive "the Spirit of truth, whom the world cannot receive, because it neither sees him nor knows him" (John 14:17). "When the Spirit of truth comes, he will guide you into all the truth; for he will not speak on his own, but will speak whatever he hears, and he will declare to you the things that are to come" (John 16: 13).

God does not want his family to be ignorant of the future. God's future plans are revealed in Scripture through divine revelation. Pastors and teachers are responsible for sharing the truth with clarity. When people feel open to share their stories, they receive the care they need. The stories that they share will be true and not general; therefore the guidance that they receive will be appropriate for them.

Another characteristic of the family of God is the sharing of material resources. People who belong to the community of believers will be people who open their hands to help others. In the ideal church, there should not be any lack in the spiritual family. Giving to assist others in need is mandatory in the family of God. Jesus indicated that family members will be blessed if they give. "Give, and it will be given to you. A good measure, pressed down, shaken together, running over, will be put into your lap; for the measure you give will be the measure you get back" (Luke 6:38).

Jesus was perfect in unity with God and the Holy Spirit. He desires that all followers who love him be perfected in unity (John 17:22-23). Jesus and his followers were an inclusive and unified group that loved one another and stuck together. According to the apostle Paul, the perfect bond of unity is love. "Above all, clothe yourselves with love, which binds everything together in perfect harmony" (Col. 3:14).

Family solidarity is important in the body of Christ. There is strength in unity. A cohesive group is stronger than a divided group. A rope made of three intertwined threads will be much stronger than each individual thread. Youth are subjected to discouragement, defeat, and depression when they are isolated and alone. The church provides a surrogate family that connects them to God and other believers.

Youth search for purpose and meaning in a world of chaos and confusion. The surrogate family helps them to identify their reason for being and how to develop the gifts and talents that God gave them. Paul explains, "There is one body and one Spirit, just as you were called to the one hope of your calling, one Lord, one faith, one baptism, one God and Father of all, who is above all, and through all and in all" (Eph. 4:4). The surrogate family is particularly helpful for youth with one custodial parent. When children learn that the whole church has the same father to call upon in good times and in bad times, they feel more united because of mutuality. The church partners with the single parents to provide a surrogate parent for the child.

Paul explains how all the members of the body have different functions, yet all are necessary to the overall function of the body (1 Cor. 12:12-13). The church as the surrogate family model helps youth understand the importance of community. The local church as a holistic community provides encouragement in Christ, consolation from love, sharing in the Spirit, compassion, and sympathy (Phil. 2:1). Paul said his joy was complete when the body of Christ was in one accord and had the same love with the same mind (Phil. 2:2). When a group has the mind of Christ, the members will be united. Unity in the surrogate family assists youth to put the puzzle of their life together, and they develop a sense of wholeness.

Jesus and the family of God enjoyed gregarious, kind, gentle, warm, and loving fellowship, spending the majority of their time together. Fellowship is an essential characteristic of the surrogate family of God. Even when disagreements and conflicts developed, Jesus was able to assist the disciples in working through their differences so that peace, harmony, and fellowship were restored.

Luke provides a vivid description of the new believers after Pentecost. "They devoted themselves to the apostles' teaching and fellowship, to the breaking of bread and the prayers" (Acts 2:42). The new believers in the early church spent every day together both inside and outside the temple in Jerusalem, praising God together "with glad and generous hearts" (Acts 2:46-47). As a result of their unity and fellowship, "the Lord added to their number those who were being saved" (Acts 2:47). Joyful and inclusive fellowship was conducive to the building of the kingdom of God.

Paul goes on to discuss the partnership and fellowship that existed between believers. "Do not be mismatched with unbelievers. For what partnership is there between righteousness and lawlessness? Or what fellowship is there between light and darkness" (2 Cor. 6:14). The rationale that Paul supplies for encouraging fellowship with other believers is that "we are the temple of the living God" (2 Cor. 6:16).

Paul also writes, "God is faithful; by him you were called into the fellowship of his Son, Jesus Christ our Lord" (1 Cor. 1:9). God created human beings for a relationship with himself, his Son, and the Holy Spirit. God is in three persons and yet one. The body of Christ is also one. The family of God was meant to be in communion and fellowship with one another.

John notes that the redeemed who are in fellowship with the Father and his Son Jesus Christ desire fellowship with one another (1 John 1:3). This fellowship among believers creates an opportunity for "the blood of Jesus his Son to cleanse us from all sin" (1 John 1:7). We have observed that believers who are in close fellowship with mature, well-grounded Christians have a greater likelihood of stronger growth in the faith.

Believers who are in fellowship with one another receive encouragement, consolation, compassion, support, sympathy, and correction. They are truly a surrogate family. God the Father provides for the family. The sisters and brothers in Christ form a community that honors God and adds to the kingdom as the early church did. The unchurched are more likely to be drawn to the church because of genuine and loving fellowship.

Most youth have never experienced anything like this in their biological family. Many come from broken homes where conflict and division is the rule; they do not feel loved and have experienced pain and disappointment in their relationships. They withdraw from family members because they have been unable to develop and maintain healthy and trusting relationships with their kindred. The church as a surrogate family provides an opportunity for children and youth to live out their purpose in a meaningful way that honors God.

The characteristics of the church as the surrogate family of God as discussed so far could be true of other associations, groups, and communities. Those people who followed Mahatma Gandhi demonstrated love, loyalty, honesty, material solidarity, social solidarity, and fellowship. Their purpose was social change. The one characteristic that distinguishes the family of God from other families, groups, and communities is holiness. The Greek term *hagiasmos* is translated as "holiness" and means sanctification or separation to God.[187] The church as the surrogate family has been called to embody holiness.

Character traits are now taught in some schools because of the universal principles. Schools other than religious institutions do not teach holiness as a way of life. The church has taught the importance of holiness from its beginning. In the second sermon of the church after Pentecost, Peter describes Jesus as the "Holy and Righteous One, the Author of life who God raised from the dead" (Acts 3:14-15). The surrogate family of God is "God's temple" where "God's Spirit dwells in each person" (1 Cor. 3:16).

Paul teaches the importance of not polluting the body or the spirit. God gave us a body, mind, and spirit that are used to glorify Him. Many youth of today take on destructive practices that cause destruction to their own parts. Their influence can lead others to follow their habits, which results in a spreading of the pollution to

---

[187] W.E. Vine, Vine's Complete Expository Dictionary of Old and New Testament Words (Nashville: Thomas Nelson, 1996), 307.

whole communities. Paul teaches, "If anyone destroys God's temple, God will destroy that person. For God's temple is holy, and you are that temple" (1 Cor. 3:17), and that clean and righteous living is essential in order to enjoy the presence of God. "Beloved, let us cleanse ourselves from every defilement of body and spirit, making holiness perfect in the fear of God" (2 Cor. 7:1).

In order to live the way of holiness, one must be properly rooted and grounded in a family with a head that connects the body together. Jesus is the cornerstone and head of the church. He built the church on the foundation of the prophets and apostles (Eph. 2:20). Paul teaches that God's family comes together and prospers as a holy vessel. "In him the whole structure is joined together and grows into a holy temple in the Lord; in whom you also are built together spiritually into a dwelling place for God" (Eph. 2:21-22).

The sacrificial element of the church as the surrogate family was made clear by Paul. "Jesus . . . loved the church and gave himself up for her, in order to make her holy by cleansing her with the washing of water by the word, so as to present the church to himself in splendor, without a spot or wrinkle or anything of the kind—yes, so that she may be holy and without blemish" (Eph. 5:25-27). Everyone wants their physical appearance to be without blemish. Jesus provides a spiritual cleansing that makes the church community whole and without blemish.

One of the characteristics of a healthy community is discipline. The family of God is disciplined by "the Father of spirits . . . for our good, in order that we may share his holiness" (Heb. 12:9-10). Peter says that the children of God are "a living stone" in the "spiritual house" and "a holy priesthood to offer spiritual sacrifices acceptable to God through Jesus Christ" (1 Pet. 2:4-5). Holiness is a prerequisite for entry into heaven (Heb. 12:14).

A life of holiness will also be a life of morality, fairness, justice, and righteousness. Life is precious and can only be lived to the fullest when it is shared with others who are not burdened by sin, destruction, and defilement. A disciplined life lived in a community leads to growth and success. The surrogate family of God works to build up the entire family. Those outside the family of God usually experience more competition than cooperation with others. Those on the inside usually experience more communion and fellowship with one another for the benefit of all. The church as the surrogate family model mentors youth in an environment that fosters collaboration, cooperation, and mutuality rather than individualism and personal competition.

Pastoral Care Theology for the Black Church as Surrogate Family

The apostle Paul states that the family of God should "Be subject to one another out of reverence for Christ" (Eph. 5:21). Aart M. van Beek suggests that the pastoral care giver use the identification processes to strengthen the care seekers identity, worldview, and sense of belonging. He recommends that the pastor build a community that identifies with the divine and fosters a sense of belonging with each other. Van Beek concludes that intercultural pastoral care must be based on intentional identification and interpathy. He defines interpathy as observing "something of the other in themselves, and vice versa."[188]

The theology of intercultural pastoral care is essential in this particular church as the surrogate family. The majority of my congregation is African American, and I am a Euro-American pastor. There are times of misunderstanding as a result of different cultural backgrounds. As a pastor I must understand my own identity, worldview, and sense of belonging before beginning to enter the world of parishioners. I work to foster mutuality and honesty in sharing around biblical stories so as to teach how all in the family of God can counteract detrimental practices and build healthy habits.

In an intercultural church family, the pastor should shepherd the congregation as a servant leader. Jesus warns the disciples that they were servants; one was not greater than another because the least in the kingdom of God was precious to God. Following the model of Jesus, the pastor is a servant and not a ruler who imposes her authority over the parishioners. Jesus is the perfect example of how a pastor should care for the other members of the surrogate family:

---

[188]   Aart M. Van Beek, *Cross- cultural Counseling in Creative Pastoral care and Counseling* (Minneapolis: Fortress Press, 1996), 76-78.

"For the Son of Man came not to be served but to serve, and to give his life a ransom for many" (Mark 10:45).

Edward P. Wimberly, in *African American Pastoral Care and Counseling: The Politics of Oppression and Empowerment*, suggests that racism, which is prevalent in society today, recruited "African Americans into negative self-images, identities, and stories."[189] He notes that the negative recruitment leads to "psychic bondage" and "internalized oppression."[190] Homer Ashby, in *Our Home Is Over Jordan*, concludes that internalized oppression was a substantial and contributing factor to the homicide rates and black-on-black crime among African Americans. Increased secularization, materialism, and isolation have also contributed to anxiety, restlessness, and unease among African Americans. Homer Ashby concludes that fragmentation, disconnection, and disassociation created a loss of a sense of community.[191]

Ashby argues that the black church was an instrument that provided care and nurture in the past and should be rediscovered in the present. He concludes that a healthy self-esteem will be recovered when the black church rediscovers the village. African Americans need a model of care and nurture that "guides interpersonal relationships, fosters love, builds compassion, constructs systems of support, and denounces violence and abuse in all forms."[192] The church as the surrogate family is a model that recreates the village of care and nurture in the community. The village of care should reduce loneliness, isolation, fragmentation, and alienation. There should also be a reduction in abuse and violence.

Edward P. Wimberly says the negative stories, identities, and images are myths based on our beliefs about ourselves. He recommends using biblical narratives to guide the editing and reauthoring of the negative myths that a person believes. When the parishioner is able

---

[189] Edward P. Wimberly, *African American Pastoral Care and Counseling: The politics of Oppression and Empowerment*, (Cleveland: The Pilgrim Press, 2006), 11.

[190] Ibid.

[191] Ibid., 19-20.

[192] Ibid., 20.

to dispel the negative myths and replace them with life-transforming stories; then healing, growth, and wholeness develop.[193] The pastoral care model in the black church as the surrogate family provides nurture, care, support, love, and compassion through interpersonal and intergenerational relationships.

Nancy Boyd-Franklin notes that the church provides relationships, advice, fellowship, spiritual support, and social activities. She therefore concludes that churches "function as surrogate families for isolated and overburdened single mothers."[194] Michael T. Mc Queen indicates that black youth need a church that is a real community: the church must be an open, loving, safe, and forgiving environment that fosters open communication and allows them to come as they are. McQueen concludes that they must be able to observe Christians in a united community that works together and shares tears and joys so that everyone grows.[195]

The church as the surrogate family has been utilized with other marginal groups that possess a duality of experience. Nanlai Cao conducted an ethnographic study with immigrant Chinese youth in a Protestant congregation in Chinatown, New York. He conducted his research from March 1999 through March 2000 at the Cantonese Church of the Lord, which originated in 1967. This particular church had evangelized among Chinese immigrant families that had recently arrived in America. The history recorded that over 50 percent of the active church were youth and young adults. Cao observed and did interviews with the pastoral leadership team, as well as with ten church members who were youth.[196]

---

193 Edward P. Wimberly, *Using Scripture in Pastoral Counseling* (Nashville: Abingdon Press, 1994), 12.

194 Nancy Boyd-Franklin, *Black Families in Therapy: Understanding the African American Experience*, 2nd ed. (New York: Guildford Press, 2003), 127-128.

195 Michael T. McQueen, "The Teens Are Watching," ed. Anne E. Streaty Wimberly, *Keep It Real: Working with Today's Black Youth* (Nashville: Abingdon Press, 2005), 105.

196 Nanlai Cao, "The Church as a Surrogate Family for Working Class Immigrant Chinese Youth: An Ethnography of Segmented Assimilation," *Sociology of Religion* 66, no. 2 (2005): 183-187.

Cao observes that the young Chinese Americans suffered from loneliness, alienation, lack of confidence, and anxiety about their futures. Their relationships with their parents were strained because of limited familial support. The strained relationships resulted in consistent conflict, tension, and frustration between the youth and their parents. The majority of the parents spoke English poorly and worked long hours at low wages. The youth received limited guidance at home, and they had freedom to seek support from their peers. One young person said that he did not have a goal and had previously gotten into trouble because he needed "something to replace the emptiness."[197]

Cao concludes that the youth population at the church was at "risk of downward assimilation to urban gang culture." The church as the surrogate family provided a feeling of empowerment, a sense of belonging, nurturing, love, and support through the intergenerational Chinese church family.[198] The intentional priestly ministry to the youth helped them overcome their negative identities, stories, and images; they were no longer potential gang members but successful and active members of the family of God.

Pastoral care that emphasizes spiritual formation as well as provides an opportunity for cultural enrichment in a nurturing surrogate church family will equip youth to deal with their stress in a healthy manner. The concept of the village has been shown to be successful with different cultural groups. Youth need an opportunity to develop healthy relationships that are built on trust. When true and intentional Christianity is fostered, youth edit and reauthor their negative myths and are transformed into a life-giving community.

Theological Conclusion

When we have communion with Jesus, we are enriched with wisdom, knowledge, and understanding of every kind. The family of

---

[197]   Ibid., 187-189.
[198]   Ibid., 197-198.

God, operating in all of the spiritual gifts, will collectively teach and practice the living, active, and powerful Word of God. We gain the mind of Christ as we yield to the *agape* (love) from God and pass it on to our sisters and brothers. Jesus strengthens and empowers the family of God. Our redemption by Jesus' death on the cross lifted us from weakness to courage, boldness, and strength.

The fellowship of Jesus can take us from inner turmoil (resulting in guilt and shame) to forgiveness, innocence, and worthiness. The holistic message of the living God raises each of us from being low and despised individuals to a noble birth as a child of the King. There should be no more sneaking and hiding in the shadows of the dark nights of our soul. There should be no more tearing down and destroying lives and relationships. With Jesus as the source of life, God is with us and for us. We are no longer individuals that are lost in a world of chaos and confusion; we are the body of Christ, united as one family whose members build up one another. The body of Christ is a vessel that Jesus developed and that God uses to bring about the process of redemption through growing sanctification, righteousness, and wisdom.

A loving committed community that embodies the truth of God's word in their relationships with one another will emulate Jesus and his disciples. They will be united for one purpose. The surrogate family of God will give of themselves and be in solidarity with others in order to build them up through the powerful and redemptive love of Jesus the Christ. The body of Christ known as the local church should be an empowered, supernatural organism that will transform the lives with which it has an interconnection.

CHAPTER THREE

Methodology for Project

The church as the surrogate family model pilot project was designed to foster a family atmosphere at Oak Chapel African Methodist Episcopal Church. The active participants of the church consist of two-thirds children and youth and one-third adults. At many of the church activities, the majority of the parents are not present. There was a need for the children and youth to have nurturing, education, and discipline in connection with spiritual education and worship. The surrogate family model was one that Jesus used with his disciples. The early church adopted the same model, but for over two thousand years the modern church has moved away from its original mission.

Theme Sermons

The church as a surrogate family was a new concept at Oak Chapel. In the past, entire families participated in worship, Sunday school, and Bible study once per week for spiritual enrichment, edification, and empowerment. In a new time and different environment, it became necessary to provide seven months that was dedicated to restoring the church to its original mission. This involved a series of seven sermons on the themes that characterize Jesus and the church as the surrogate family. Each month from June 2010 through December 2010, I shared a message on one of the seven themes.

The sermon series began in June 2010 with a message on the importance of love in the family of God. In July a sermon on loyalty, faithfulness, and commitment was provided to the church. Truth and honesty was the theme in August. The word of God is a guide for daily living and interaction with one another. In September a sermon on material solidarity with giving and sharing with one another was provided. A concrete demonstration of tithing was included as an illustration. The importance of unity and solidarity was emphasized in October through a sermon and other interactive exercises. A message on fellowship was provided in November, and the series concluded with a sermon on holiness in December.

The seven sermons were delivered in a manner different from the usual and customary practice at the church. Prior to this series, most sermons were delivered from the pulpit. Oak Chapel was built in the late 1860s. As an African Methodist Episcopal Church of that period, there are three levels. There is the floor level where the congregation sits and comes to the semicircular rail to kneel and pray. On the next level is the communion table with an open Bible, a cross, and two candles on each side of the cross; the invitation to Christian discipleship is given from this level. The third level is where the clergy leads the worship service from behind the sacred desk. This physical layout of the sanctuary is consistent with the hierarchical structure of the African Methodist Episcopal Church.

Each of the monthly theme sermons were delivered from the floor level of the sanctuary, outside of the altar rail, from behind a portable lectern within five feet of the first pew. The youth were invited to sit on the first and second pews so that they could participate in the sermon. The African method of preaching involves a call and response; each of these sermons provided several opportunities to respond. I attempted to create a family atmosphere with an interactive dialogue to facilitate retention and to encourage active participation. The congregation was encouraged to listen to the message, observe the demonstrations, and participate in the sermon in a variety of ways.

The youth were given quotes from African Americans of distinction, Scriptures, poems, and other literature to read from the lectern. The purpose of the one- to two-minute readings was used to reinforce positive images of African Americans in order to nurture, enlighten, and enhance their identity as African American youth.

Specific quotes and contributions were used to support the sermon theme for the month. The African American Church as a surrogate family was highlighted each sermon to demonstrate how each theme was a necessary part of the church family structure and function. At some time during the sermon, I would make the point that being a part of God's family brings health, healing, and wholeness. We are all interconnected and depend upon God and one another to achieve true success. God's family as modeled by Jesus sets the standard, not our biological family.

Each theme sermon was an opportunity for them to experience the church as the surrogate family. Members were encouraged to make the theme topic a part of their own life. Every sermon challenged the congregation to develop a deeper understanding and manifestation of the theme topic in their own relationship with God and with others. Practical examples were provided from Scriptures, African American heritage, and daily experiences to stimulate further thought and practice. The key goal was always transformation rooted in orthopraxis from an individual orientation (I and me) to a family and community thought (we and our). We tried to facilitate the development of positive, holistic, and new attitudes through theological concepts and principles.

Family Fun Night and Bible Studies

Next, I attempted to foster practical theology in functional ways by facilitating the development of new attitudes. How do new attitudes develop within spiritual groups? We believe that one must be nurtured in their faith in God through discipleship as Jesus nurtured the disciples. In order to become disciples, we must be born anew of God's Spirit and of water. We are restored to God's original design for us through healing from our inward being. Everything becomes new from a spiritual perspective, which brings new light to our minds and new strength for our bodies.

The new spirit must now be sustained by the words of Jesus. The church as God designed it provides sustenance for the spirit, mind, and body. We spend at least five hours per week learning about God and His principles for living. At God's house we eat together as Jesus and

His disciples did as often as possible. As we walk together, the great shepherd and the under-shepherds guide the youth within healthy boundaries through gentle and kind prodding and directing. This involved rewarding healthy interactions with positive reinforcement and unhealthy interactions with time out and counseling. This process of sustaining and guiding takes time, humility, and patience; this is best accomplished when the church as the surrogate family follows the example of Jesus and walks in His pathway.

Through this process, a new attitude develops as a result of reconciliation with God through Jesus the Christ. Once we are reconciled with God, a desire develops and grows to become reconciled with others through God's grace. We are enriched, empowered, and encouraged to move forward by faith to reconcile all relationships through the Holy Spirit. Those who have suffered from poverty, racism, classism, sexism, violence, degradation, exploitation, and dehumanization can become whole through a holistic process of nurturing when the necessary social supports are in place.

The other activities that were used to reinforce the concept of the church as the surrogate family was a series of seven Bible studies and family fun nights that replaced the usual Wednesday night Bible study once per month. Those special Bible studies were usually held at the end of the month after the monthly theme sermon had been provided. In the past year the church had studied the biblical books of Daniel and Revelation during Wednesday night Bible study. During the seven-month period, the church would have an interactive study of a chapter of Revelation on the first three Wednesday nights.

The church provides a birthday celebration for each member or frequent attendant on the Wednesday night nearest their birthday. A birthday cake with drinks and chips is always shared with all who are present. The birthday parties have been a part of the Wednesday night Bible studies for three years. The focus during the seven months was centered on the value of each person to the family of God. The ministers took the opportunity to nurture and foster each person's unique gifts and talents. This was a time of encouragement for their growth and development over the past year. The theme for this activity is that each person is unique. David writes, "For it was you who formed my inward parts; you knit me together in my mother's womb.

I praise you, for I am fearfully and wonderfully made. Wonderful are your works that I know very well" (Ps. 139: 13-14).

Each Bible study and Family Fun Night was designed based on an African village model; these were intergenerational meetings that were held in a circle. Both youth and adults were provided Scripture for a short Bible lesson lasting approximately fifteen minutes. Following the Bible lesson, those assembled were encouraged to share their stories. The church provided musical instruments for each person to play as a part of a musical selection at the beginning and end of each session. Each person who had a story to share with the group came to the center and played a few notes on the African drum and shared the story. This was done outside in July and August and in the church basement at other times.

The goal of this activity was to teach and to promote the importance of members' African heritage. A secondary goal was to assist the youth, particularly in articulating their stories for the benefit of the family of God. These sessions provided them an opportunity to discuss their concerns and have a dialogue with the elders about issues with which they were struggling. Most of the dialogue centered on current issues. The importance of the interconnection of the family of God provides the wisdom, support, and encouragement to make informed decisions about things that we all face on a daily basis. Our past successes and failures are behind us, and we can reauthor our stories by making new informed decisions that build relationships and promote maturity.

A safe, supportive, and sustaining church environment allows the youth to work through their issues because they can ask their questions and hear from many voices. Youth often approach difficult concerns from an indirect position. The many sources of information are brought together so that they can select alternative solutions from those discussed without shame, embarrassment, or ridicule. These sessions promote a biblical worldview in the reality of today's world. Some might call these activities rap sessions or talk-back sessions, but I prefer to call them an interactive dialogue between youth, ministerial leaders, and other adults. The purpose of the seven sessions was to facilitate nurturing, and the church used Edward P. Wimberly's pastoral care model of healing, sustaining, guiding, and reconciling as a practical tool.

The first session that occurred in June introduced the Church as the surrogate family. The Scripture that was provided was Mark 3:31-35. Various youth volunteered to read the verses from the New Revised Standard Version and also read Mark 3:21 in order to place the Scripture in context. We explained that Jesus' family tried to rescue him because they thought that he had delusions of grandeur and was out of his mind. Jesus was not understood by his biological family because the family had not been enlightened nor empowered by the Spirit of God. We discussed what it must have been like for Jesus to experience rejection and misunderstanding from his natural family. We can identify with Jesus because we feel rejected and misunderstood some of the time.

I asked the question, "What does it take to do the will of God?" The youth volunteered what they thought about doing the will of God. The discussion lasted thirty minutes and covered the seven important characteristics of the family of God. We compared and contrasted the natural family and the spiritual family. A question was asked about how brothers and sisters in Christ communicate and behave toward one another. Because we are all sisters and brothers, there should be a spirit of sharing and cooperation with one another. There should not be any offensive language, communication, or touching between spiritual family members. Those who do the will of God are the ones who are wise, inspired, and empowered to be channels of Jesus' love, grace, and power.

We discussed the difference between individualism represented by I, me, and mine versus being a part of a community represented by we, us, and our. The dialogue began with a Yoruba proverb: "He who has the support of others can achieve great things." We were created to thrive with communal support. Those who become isolated and separated will often experience emptiness. Anger and rebellion that is not discussed in healthy ways will often be acted out in unhealthy ways. Jesus the healer works through the church universal to restore and renew the souls of community participants. The church as the surrogate family can be a community healer when it enters into solidarity with those who struggle with violence and abuse. The church also provides a forum for expression and processing of painful experiences in a loving, nurturing, and supportive community. The family of God is trustworthy when it works as Jesus intended for it to work.

At the end of the first session, I passed out the words to a song that was adopted by a Chinese American church in New York entitled "Our Family."

> We are one family in the Living Lord,
> We are one family in the Living Lord,
> Let us join our spirits, with the Spirit of God,
> We are one family in the Living Lord.
> We are one in the bond of love,
> Let us sing Now, ev'ry one,
> Let us feel His love begun,
> Let us join our hands that the world will know,
> We are one Family in the Living Lord.[199]

After we read the song together in unison, we formed a circle and held hands for our closing prayer. This was followed by the celebration of the birthday of one of our youth who was eighteen. Each month, the pastor selected a song that would be sung throughout the month.

The second session was delayed until the first week of August because of the hospitalization of the pastor's husband. This was the first outdoor session. The Scripture lesson was Galatians 3:23-4:7, which had been printed from the NRSV and passed out. A local minister joined us and brought bells and African drums for all of the children to play; one of the youth played a selection on his trumpet. The emphasis was equality in the family of God. No one is more important than another because we are all heirs and are one in Christ Jesus.

We all have experiences, testimonies, and stories that can provide encouragement to another in their time of difficulty. Testimonies are used more frequently in the AME Church than in some other mainline denominations. Much of the support for those in slavery came in the form of oral testimonies and stories that were passed

---

[199]   Nanlai Cao, "The Church as the Surrogate Family," 183-198.

down through the generations. The sharing of testimonies and stories helps to facilitate open communication within the group.

This session was a time of great sharing by children, youth, and adults. The storytelling lasted for approximately thirty minutes. There were many stories about successful achievements to encourage the children and youth who were returning to school in a few days. This was truly an African-style intergenerational sharing intended to provide inspiration, motivation, and support for the children and youth in the upcoming academic term. After the prayer circle for a successful school year, the entire group shared in returning the chairs and instruments to the church basement.

At the end of August, we conducted the third session and held it outside with the chairs in a circle. The Scripture lesson was from Romans 8:28-39. The Bible lesson was read by the children and then discussed, with emphasis on the love of God in Christ Jesus. The purpose of this session was to promote self-worth. There was a discussion about the power of God's love; we can count on Jesus, who is our intercessor, and nothing can separate us from his love. We had two experts in African names and stories that shared the meaning of certain names.

Even when our natural families let us down and disappoint us, we know that we all have one Father who loves us and will never forsake us. Our Father has a very important purpose for each of us to fulfill. We are made in the image of God, and God desires for us to be conformed to the image of His son. Jesus is our brother and the firstborn in our large family. He has given us resurrection power so that we are more than conquerors. The power of His love is so great that we, as his sisters and brothers, are empowered to counteract negative influences and the evil that is in the world. This session included African drumming and a prayer circle.

In September we followed up on the idea of image and identity. The youth indicated that they wanted us to have a session on tattoos and body piercing; this session was conducted by another minister of the church, and she shared various Scriptures to provide insight regarding the subject. Some things in the Bible are compulsory, and other things are a matter of one's judgment based on biblical principles. The moral law of the New Testament based on the Old Testament must be obeyed. Other things such as drinking a glass of wine would be permitted because it is not prohibited in the New Testament. She placed tattoos and body piercings in the category of preference, as long as they were done in moderation. She led the discussion by having the participants respond to various statements which were provided on a handout.

There was a lively discussion about the body being the temple of God. In the Old Testament God commanded, "You shall not make any cuts in your body for the dead nor make any tattoo marks on yourselves: I am the Lord" (Lev. 19:28). God's family is called to be holy and blameless; they are to be set apart from the world and consecrated for God's purposes. A tattoo makes a permanent and indelible mark on our bodies that were made in the image of God. Paul instructed Christians to "present your bodies as a living sacrifice, holy and acceptable to God, which is your spiritual worship. Do not be conformed to this world, but be transformed by the renewing of your minds, so that you may discern what is the will of God—what is good and acceptable and perfect" (Rom. 12:1-2).

The session in October was conducted by the pastor on the topic of bullying. The Scripture was printed from James 4:1-4 and distributed to all participants. Two additional Scriptures were read by various children. Paul stated, "But if you bite and devour one another, take care that you are not consumed by one another" (Gal. 5:15). Peter commanded, "Honor everyone. Love the family of believers. Fear God" (1 Pet. 2:17). A series of questions were asked. Why do dogs fight? Why do children bite other children? Why do people fuss and fight? The children were invited to answer the questions first, because this was focused more toward children twelve and under. The reasons for violence and rebellion can be a desire for control, attention, or significance. There could be an unmet need of some sort. According to James chapter four, they act out by assaulting others because they did not get their way. These are a few of the many reasons why people respond with violence and rebellion.

Two quotes were provided to share insight on the causes of bullying. Cornel West writes in *Race Matters* that many African Americans destroy other people and themselves because they lack three essential things: love, hope, and meaning. When trust is violated through abandonment, rejection, and abuse, the trauma leaves scars that alter one's ability to form and sustain healthy relationships.[200] Coretta Scott King, an American civil rights activist, said "There is no problem that can't be solved if we can corral our resources behind it. That means people, that means money, that means the good will and cooperation of a large segment of the people."[201]

We discussed the resources that each child and young person had when they were bullied. They had teachers, parents, and ministers that they could talk to about anything that bothers them. The church should create safe spaces where youth can be free of bullying. The adult leaders in the church should be proactive against bullying. Children also had an opportunity to pray to God for help in their situation. The Bible provides guidance about how they should deal with bullies: they should pray for them and seek to be a light by not retaliating. Many problems can be resolved through civil dialogue. When we discuss our concerns through open communication, we are more likely to hear more desirable alternative solutions. The Holy Spirit is the true guide who draws out the desired solution.

We explained that hate-filled words and conduct are like rocks thrown at other people—they reveal something about the heart of the thrower: there is something missing from the thrower's heart. People may be aggressive and extremely competitive, because they are insecure and lack self-confidence. We ended with a discussion of child abuse reporting requirements for church officials. Child abuse is an extreme form of adult bullying. We concluded with a prayer circle for those who had been silenced by bullies.

The November special Bible Study and Family Fun Night included a special Thanksgiving dinner and service that was conducted by a ministry couple from Oklahoma City. The Scriptures that were presented were Philippians 3:1 and 4:4-7, and Matthew 7:7-8, 11. This session began with praise and worship music from a DVD produced by Israel Houghton. The congregation was invited to sing along with our guest music minister.

---

[200] Cornel West, *Race Matters*, 23.

[201] Quinn Eli, ed., *African-American Wisdom* (Philadelphia: Running Press, 1996), 72.

We should rejoice in the Lord at all times. We do not like it when we are mistreated, but we must rejoice that we know Jesus and the power of his resurrection. Children of God can rejoice that they shine like stars in this crooked and perverse generation. The surrogate family of God can rejoice because they hold fast to the Word of Life.

God is our provider. We must ask in faith and trust God to provide for our needs. Unfortunately, some parents are unable to provide food for hungry children and youth due to a lack of resources. Our parents do not usually give us a rock when we are hungry. We are God's children, and He loves us with an indescribable love. God wants to give us great gifts. God wants to do more for us than we can ever expect. God blesses those who are obedient to His will. A faithful person will receive good things from God. Paul said, "And my God will fully satisfy every need of yours according to his riches in glory in Christ Jesus" (Phil. 4:19); this lesson taught patience, persistence, and faith. Jesus summarized the key by saying, "But strive first for the kingdom of God and his righteousness, and all these things will be given to you as well" (Matt. 6:33). This session ended with an invitation to become a Christian and a prayer circle.

The final session was on God's promises, which are realized through faith. The Scripture from Romans 4: 13-25 was printed and passed out to all participants. The emphasis was on the unity of the family of God through faith. Abraham was justified by faith before he was circumcised. Abraham is the father of all who believe in God by faith; he was absolutely convinced that God would keep His promises. Paul said, "Therefore his faith was reckoned to him as righteousness" (Rom. 4:22). We are justified by faith in Jesus.

Because this was the last Bible Study and Family Fun night for the year and for the series, we discussed our goals for the future. We asked a series of questions in relationship to the subject of putting our faith into action. Based on what has been taught about the church as the surrogate family, how do you plan to exercise your faith differently in 2011? Everyone had an opportunity to discuss their own views and potential changes that they would like to make in the future. The interactive dialogue lasted approximately thirty minutes.

During the month of December 2010, the youth of the church constructed banners with the guidance and direction of the ministers. The pastor agreed to give twenty-five dollars to each young person who designed and decorated a theme banner. Children were provided with a square yard of four different colors of felt. They used a one-foot portion of each piece of felt to cut out letters and designs to place on each banner. The word that most accurately represented the theme discussed was placed on the banner. These banners were hung on dowels and hung in the sanctuary during the rest of the conference year, and they were presented to the church after they were completed as a summation of the themes that characterize the church as the surrogate family.

The children's minister designed a beautiful hunter green banner to represent the children's ministry. There were two large brown acorns on each side near the bottom. The banner had the name Oak Chapel AME Church at the top with the word "acorns" beneath the church name. The banner had the name Children's Ministry below the acorns. The letters were all in white, which provided a wonderful contrast. The children each signed their names on the back. There were approximately ten children actively involved in the children's ministry at the end of the project.

The church provided similar survey and interview tools at the beginning and end of the project. All of the surveys were initially completed during a time prior to Sunday school on Sunday morning. The project had previously been shared with the church at the church conference. At the initial church conference, people asked questions and shared any concerns. After an interactive dialogue and explanations from the pastor, the church members unanimously agreed to participate. The pastor specifically spoke to the parents of younger children to obtain their consent for their children to be involved in the church as the surrogate family project.

CHAPTER FOUR

Project Evaluations

The Church as the Surrogate Family model impacted Oak Chapel AME Church in a positive way. The greatest accomplishment was that three parents of the children accepted Jesus as their Savior and committed themselves to discipleship and church membership. The original theme of love combined with the teaching on sisters and brothers in Christ seemed to set the tone for changes in attitudes, communications, and behavior. The model worked well for a small African American congregation that consisted of two-thirds children and youth. The members that had been in church all of their lives were not as appreciative of the sermon series and the Family Fun Night series as those who had been active members two to three years.

Survey Results and Observations

The findings of this limited pilot project were similar to the study involving Chinese American youth in New York. The real key to changing behavior in a spiritual context is clearly love and nurturing; the cultural context does not seem to make a significant difference. Most people respond positively to love and nurturing. Edward P. Wimberly's model of healing, sustaining, guiding, and reconciling provided the framework for the orthopraxis used in this model. His model worked extremely well with Joseph Hellerman's model of the church as the surrogate family. Hellerman, Hunt, and Mucherera provided the theology, and Wimberly demonstrated the orthopraxis of how those concepts could be implemented in an African American congregation.

A survey was conducted in the beginning of the project to determine whether the individuals had a more individualistic perspective as opposed to a community perspective. Approximately half of the group started with high values for a community perspective. Approximately 25 percent felt that they were more alone, which indicated a more individualistic perspective. Over 80 percent indicated that they had a deep obligation to the church. Only two people had an ambivalent commitment to the church.

Approximately half of the people surveyed voiced a desire to be more committed to the church community. One person said she wanted to be able to shut out distractions. An ideal description of the church as the surrogate family as described by Joseph Hellerman was provided, and they were asked if it appealed to them. Approximately 70 percent said that it was appealing and that they would want to be a part of a church with those conditions. The advantages listed were that the church would provide protection for the individual. Advantages for the church as a whole were listed as: love, unity, commitment, a positive influence on members, improved likelihood of evangelism, help with life decisions, help to grow spiritually, and help for everyone to reach a common goal. They unanimously agreed that the church as family helped to inform their concept of brothers and sisters in Christ.

The project began on June 1, 2010, and by July 2010 we were observing positive and healthy changes in the behavior of the youth. There had been some challenges between an eleven-year-old boy and two older boys during May and June. In July eight children went to a four-day youth conference in Hampton, Virginia. The group consisted of four teen girls, two teen boys, and two smaller boys. I observed that the two teen boys helped the two younger boys with their hair and grooming. One eighteen-year-old teen said, "I am trying to make them look good." The younger boys liked the attention and improved in their appearance. During the various activities, I observed how close they had grown. The teen boy cared for the two younger boys like they were his brothers; there was no conflict between them that we observed.

After returning from the youth conference, we did not observe conflict but only cooperation between the boys. The older boy said that the emphasis on the surrogate family of God "made me more considerate of others" and "made me think of others more." He began to exercise leadership skills among the other youth and often served as a spokesperson for the youth in his new leadership capacity during the rest of the year. I observed him serving in the church and sharing with the others. He came to understand the importance of love and unity.

At the first outdoor family fun night, we observed that the younger children were more focused and attentive when they were given musical instruments to play such as bells, drums, and tambourines. They listened attentively when the older youth and adults told their stories of how they achieved significant success in school, the military, and in life in general. There were stories of how some of the adults struggled to go to college when schools and society was segregated. There were stories of how taking the hard courses and the harder teachers in high school paid off in preparation for college. One young person said she was the first in her family to finish high school and go to college.

Overall the stories were extremely encouraging for the younger teens and children. At the end of the project, all the children twelve and under who had been active in the church were dreaming of going to college. A college-bound student had been the preschool Sunday school teacher for eight months prior to leaving for college. The four younger children cried because they wanted her to stay with them. Even though they were upset initially, we could observe their growth and development as a result of her nurturing and caring personality. She did a poster with all the symbols for each theme for the preschoolers. The poster was placed on the wall above their table where they met for Sunday school and Bible study.

The Sunday school superintendent noticed that the children were being creative and talking in front of the entire Sunday school. Before the project started, they would not discuss their review in front of the group; they often held their heads down and let the teacher do all the talking; they talked during their lesson but not in front of the other classes. During the project, they began holding up their papers, showing what they had colored or drawn, and they answered questions about the lesson. During this time none of their parents attended Sunday school. The children received considerable nurturing from the adults and older teens.

Each second Sunday is youth day, and the teens participate in the worship service. Unfortunately the teens prefer not to do the morning prayer. The pastor asked if any young person would like to offer the prayer. A six-year-old boy raised his hand. Immediately we heard the teens saying, "Boy, put your hand down." The pastor invited the child to the altar rail, and the two of them knelt together. The child prayed the most wonderful prayer. He was very sincere in asking God to help all the children to act like good children and to keep the devil away from them. The gentle sustaining and guiding that had occurred in the church prepared him so that he felt comfortable praying for the entire congregation.

The first sermon on love was the most helpful to the majority of people. Eighty percent of the ten people interviewed at the completion of the project identified love as their favorite and most meaningful theme. Throughout the seven months we observed many examples of love being demonstrated in the church. The church has three active adult males, and two of them were assigned children's Sunday school classes starting in August. I often observed them tying shoes, comforting an upset child, and providing guidance and discipline to the children. They each, in their own special way, were instruments of God's will. In some cases they were truly fathers to the fatherless.

On one occasion the church took the children and youth to the North Carolina state fair. When the person running the fair activity seemed to be taking advantage of the younger boys, one of the men stepped up and intervened. When a ride required an adult with a boy on a go cart, one of our men shared those moments with him. They have discipled the boys in our church and have demonstrated God's love in many ways. Most of the children come from an environment where there is not a father consistently in the home. The children respond well to the men's instruction and guidance. We believe that it was this nurturing environment that led the children to trust Jesus as their personal savior; they learned that they could trust the adults in the church, and therefore they could trust God, who is the father of us all.

The children and youth were very active in the church fall revival, most of them attending all three nights. The first two nights we had invited men to preach the sermon. The third night we invited a former pastor of the church who is female. One of the children who stood in front of me while the Oak Chapel choir sang the special selection kept turning his head to look at our guest preacher in the pulpit. When she finished the sermon and gave the benediction, the child went running into the pulpit to hug her. He had never met her before, but he figured she was one of us now, and he could trust her.

The teens said that they liked the quotes from African Americans that they read each time we had a theme sermon. We noticed they began to stand up straight and read louder and clearer when they read about famous African Americans. We observed growth and development in their identity and self-worth. All of the teen girls stated that many of the exercises helped them with their self-confidence. We also noticed a willingness to serve and volunteer to help care for the younger children. When we traveled as a church family, we observed them taking the hand of a younger child. They made sure the young ones got their food and went to the restroom.

We have a baby in our church that just turned one in December 2010. I have observed everyone in the entire church holding the baby; the teens particularly enjoy caring for her. The small children likewise seem to want to sit with whoever was holding the baby. The church as the surrogate family has drawn us closer together as a church family. We are more united and work together more now than when we started the project in June.

We are beginning to see the needs of others and reach out to meet those needs. As we grew as a church family, we also reached out to the people in the community. One of our church leaders who lived near the church would visit the sick and elderly every week. Our church attendance grew dramatically during the seven months. During the last night of vacation Bible school, we had twenty children and youth. The entire church went into the community to invite people to come to Oak Chapel on October 31, 2010. During November and December, we often had between twenty and thirty people, mostly children and youth for Bible study on Wednesday night.

One of our adult leaders said that the family night circle gatherings outside "showed the community the closeness of the church family." Because of the closeness of the church family, other families in the community have expressed interest in coming to the church. We added a total of six people to our church family over the seven-month period. We also had an additional ten conversions that occurred at the Thanksgiving fellowship Bible study in November. We received two large contributions at the end of December from people who observed our ministry from a distance and wanted to sow seeds into it.

When our church participated in other church services in town, we received positive feedback on how well behaved our teens were during the worship service. We received approximately thirty United Methodist hymnals from another church during the seven months. We also received an anonymous African American framed stamp collection during this time. Several people who appreciate African American heritage activities stopped by on Wednesday nights to assist us with the Family Fun Nights. Our emphasis on the church as the surrogate family enhanced goodwill and community within the larger community. Our interaction with other churches has facilitated more openness with churches in town.

The majority of active members interviewed or surveyed stated that all the sermons and Bible studies were helpful, and they did not find any of them unhelpful or uninformative. Two or three indicated that the sermon on truth was their least favorite. One person liked the topical studies more than the scriptural based studies that expounded on the church as the surrogate family. Several people indicated the emphasis on unity was helpful. The interactive dialogue that occurred during the theme sermons was lively. Adults and youth seemed more attentive during theme sermons and often responded when pastors asked questions of the congregation.

According to one of the associate ministers, the project helped to foster her identity in Christ. One other person noted that her family had not been to church for a long period of time prior to them becoming members of our church. She indicated that the themes really helped her to understand how to live the Christian life; the project facilitated her Christian growth and maturity. She commented that her identity in Christ had transformed the way she made decisions and who she sought out as friends. When she arrived at a United

Methodist college for African American women, she sought upper-class people to pray with her. She soon became one of the first-year students that other students would come to for assistance.

One person stated that she felt that the church family was more supportive of goals to pursue higher education than her biological family. The message that God loves everyone the same was important to several of the youth. Belonging to the church helped one person overcome sadness from the loss of a relationship. The church as the surrogate family helped the youth to become more open to people who were different from them. The teaching on God as Father was extremely important to those children and youth who had lost a parent.

Reflections of the Church as the Surrogate Family

The church as a surrogate family is not perfect. As our church family grew, there have been some growing pains. The ministerial team had to teach the original children and youth to be friendly to the newcomers. When new groups of children came, they sat together, and the original group sat in a group. We attempted to facilitate more involvement and interaction by dividing the Bible study into four groups. They were asked to count off so that they would be in small discussion groups with different people. The junior class seemed to grow and work together with the new people within a few weeks due to some creative socialization activities that their teacher put in place.

The pastor has administrative weaknesses and is not as organized as she should be. One person stated that the guest speakers were not adequately briefed regarding the purpose of the Family Fun Night sessions. One guest came prepared to assist the teens in writing their stories. On the night in question there were three adults, three teens, and several younger children in attendance with two guest participants. The largest group was four or five younger children. In a volunteer church setting, one never knows who will be there, and therefore the pastor has to be flexible. We had a good session about the importance of African names, but it was more helpful to the younger children.

In retrospect the majority of the church was in agreement with the project, but one person had reservations from the beginning. The majority of the church was supportive and cooperative. This model would, therefore, work better with churches that are more youth oriented rather than churches without many children. The more conservative, established churches would probably find the model more challenging. Some people would not be content to care for other people's children. Those with a more individualistic perspective would be expected to resist a community and family model for their church.

The church as the surrogate family model requires an investment of time and talents. This model certainly requires sacrifice on the part of the adults and ministers involved, but the rewards are tremendous. Oak Chapel had an open door to minister to the families of the children that were active in the church. The grandmother of one child expressed her gratitude for all the church was doing for her grandchildren. She said the children sing "Jesus Loves Me" and "This Little Light of Mine" at home. She said that one day she planned to visit our church. The children and youth express so much love and give the adults so much joy.

The churches that have been influenced by Western values would probably have more difficulty with the focus on African principles and African American history. People who value the village of care would probably be more open to using circular seating arrangements that foster unity and inclusivity. The Western model uses more lecturing and teaching, with the teacher at the front and the participants in neat little rows. In a community model everyone is important, and what they say is valued by the entire group.

African-oriented models employ creative forms of expression that invite participation. The gospel music, dance, and biblical drama help to integrate the message and make it more a part of one's own life. When various instruments are used in praise and worship, it reinforces rhythm and harmony. When a song of the month supports the theme, it facilitates and enhances unity as the church sings together. Involvement produces more retention than just listening or observing. The common call and response used in African American churches makes the experience more interactive and memorable. This church as the surrogate family model uses culture to enhance worship, Bible study, and Sunday school. According to the comments by most of the church family, my thesis was supported: the church as the surrogate family model impacted Oak Chapel AME Church in a healthy way.

CHAPTER FIVE

CONCLUSION AND RECOMMENDATIONS

We end where we began, knowing that Jesus has provided us the best model. He has demonstrated through his practical theology how to be the church. The model has not changed in two thousand years, but each culture will express its theology in a different manner. Jesus is eternal, and his steadfast love endures forever; He has shown us how to receive people into the kingdom of God and nurture them as our brothers and sisters. First, we must be willing to surrender our hearts to God so that the Holy Spirit may guide and direct our hands to lift others up through good works.

We asked the question whether the church as the surrogate family can impact our congregation. We have answered yes. We recognize that not every church will agree to accept the necessary sacrifices to implement this model. Even though this was a simple, brief, and small project in a rural African American church in North Carolina, we believe that it has the essential theological principles and the orthopraxis to be replicated with any church in any culture.

Highlights of Oak Chapel History

We have learned that God's love is so powerful that it calls us to work for justice against the dehumanization of slavery. As we attempted to examine the history of Oak Chapel, we discovered the atrocities, horrors, exploitation, and oppression that occurred by the intentional action of greedy, evil, and sinful people. As we read the slanted and narrow-minded views of local historians, we were shocked and saddened that 150 years after slavery, some hearts were still filled with disgust and bitterness for the freedmen's children.

As we interviewed local people that we believed had information about the history of Oak Chapel, we observed many tears and much sadness for the centuries of mistreatment that occurred in Warren County, North Carolina. When we asked why nothing good was recorded about the church, even though it has been in existence for so long, the church's eldest member said, "We were treated as if we were not important." There was a total disregard and disrespect for the founders of the church even though most of them achieved unprecedented success considering the hardships that they endured.

Reconstructing Oak Chapel's history was like putting a puzzle together. Certain facts had not been recorded in the local history books. The Great Migration hindered the recording of African American history on the local level because so many people migrated north. The church is located near a spring and experienced many floods that destroyed church records.

When the pieces came together, a wonderful image emerged. Those who founded the church and served in leadership capacities were giants in the faith; they overcame insurmountable obstacles to achieve success. They became great educators, politicians, actors, preachers, and highly skilled craftsmen. Oak Chapel has truly served well and has a proud history.

Many excellent brick-and-rock masons and carpenters were involved in building and restoring Oak Chapel over its long history. Because of their superior skill and knowledge, they built a church that stands proudly on its original foundation, when all other churches built during that time for African Americans in Warrenton have ceased to exist. Outstanding preachers and pastors have served the church through the years. Because of all who have served and contributed to God's work, many people have been saved, delivered, healed, and transformed. Oak Chapel has been the church as the surrogate family to hundreds of thousands of young people over the course of its history.

The church has remained true to its original mission to serve the people of the community. Even though Warren County has gone from prosperity and wealth to poverty in the past 150 years, the community the church served has always been oppressed and poor in spirit—they were newly freed slaves and free people who had limited education, material resources, and political power. Oak Chapel continues to thrive because it never lost the vision that God gave to the founders, who were determined to have a place where they could freely worship God.

They understood rejection and mistreatment, and they welcomed Native Americans, who had no place to worship. They loved and nurtured those who were poor and downtrodden. Their chief goal has been to provide spiritual, educational, and economic foundations for community members. They have led the community in the areas of social justice and human rights. I see similarities between the poor of Africa and the poor of Warrenton. We all need love, hope, and meaning. Jesus walked through villages and visited homes so that He could heal, sustain, guide, and reconcile people who were adrift without direction. He constantly loves and nurtures people, so that we can grasp the vision of who He really is.

Lingering Effects of Poverty and Racism Results in Nihilism

Many African Americans have experienced feelings of inferiority, rejection, and mistreatment by whites. The feeling of being unwanted takes a toll on the spirit, soul, and mind. I am convinced that early violations of trust such as abuse, neglect, and affliction cause trauma and scarring that only Jesus can heal. Poverty and racism has been shown to have a profound effect on people. The constant lack of resources to meet basic human needs, in conjunction with the degradation and dehumanization of racism, can cause deep-seated pain. Repeated assaults on one's integrity, character, and existence can create inner anger and despair. There can be a profound sense of loss when a person is treated in an unequal manner.

Constant and repeated threats, assaults, and affronts can lead to loss and emptiness. This treatment can result in feelings of hopelessness, lovelessness, and meaninglessness. People may experience one of two reactions. Some feel constantly anxious because they try to counteract the inferiority with achievement. Feelings that one is not good enough to meet others' expectations can foster self-doubt. Sometimes high achievers fit into this category; there is an inner desire to be somebody.

Some cope with the pain by using drugs, alcohol, sex outside of marriage, and other means of escape. The combination of the inner rage, rebellion, poverty, and substance abuse makes it difficult to maintain relationships. Feelings of being attacked from within and without can create a sense of alienation that leads to isolation. Some experience fragmentation and deteriorate into confusion and despair. Some flee family and community due to bombardment with reminders about their failure and loss. A few end up homeless and on the streets of large urban cities.

Parents who work long hours to support a family on one income need support and partnership from the church family. Children come into the world expecting love, nurture, and sustenance. When their expectations are not met due to overwhelming circumstances, the child's trust can be violated. Some of them experience the same or similar pain, loss, shame, and anger that their family before them experienced. In some cases they lack the necessary resources needed to grow and develop and be made whole.

Some parents without a family support system or church family have little time or energy to provide nurturing, guidance, and discipline for their children. Healing of the inner pain and rage can come from Jesus and His church. The church as the surrogate family appears to be part of the solution. The church was created to minister to the poor, the oppressed, the blind, and those bound by sin and other destructive forces. All people need assistance in becoming reconciled to God. The church must reach out beyond its four walls and become partners with the parents who are struggling with poverty and racism.

The children cannot wait for their parents to pull themselves up by their bootstraps and bring the family to church. The church must go to the parents and offer them some respite care in the form of love and nurturing. Even very small children will learn to trust the adults in the church when they demonstrate the love of Jesus. The more love and nurturing the church provides, the more impact they will have on the child and their family. The families learn that they can overcome racism and poverty through reconciliation with God through Jesus the Christ. Some will receive healing through the weekly sustenance and guidance provided by the body of Christ. Churches that choose to become the surrogate family will be instruments of transformation.

We are all created in the image of God. Unfortunately our images become distorted through sin and evil. Jesus redeems and empowers us so that we can be conformed to God's image and likeness. The scarring of our image through poverty and racism results in insults to our identity and self-worth. The church as the surrogate family helps to renew our self-image and sense of value. Jesus enters our heart and renews and restores our spirit and mind. The family of God, operating fully with the spiritual gifts, helps to identify the areas of our stories that need revision. The myths can be renounced and our stories reauthored to reflect God's image. We can walk in our new image and live according to God's will when we have reauthored our central story. In some cases relationships can be reconciled so that people can live together in peace and harmony.

Part of the renewal process occurs through education and enlightenment. In order to function as the family of God, the church must come to understand the essential characteristics of God's family. As the church studies what God's love looks like, the Holy Spirit will demonstrate the power of God's love through the church family. God's faithfulness is highlighted to help new family members understand the importance of loyalty and commitment to God and His family. The truth of God's Word serves to sustain and guide us through the transformation process. We can learn that God's family is giving. Material solidarity and unity should provide the necessary support so that people do not feel isolated and alone. The one body of Christ is united in fellowship and holiness when it functions properly. When members understand and practice all seven themes, the church more accurately reflects the image of God.

Follow-up on the Practical Theology Model

The question should be asked about what type of follow-up will be provided to prepare the children and youth for a successful future.

Education, enrichment, and empowerment are an ongoing process. The three African Methodist denominations met approximately one year ago to discuss the best methods to assist African American youth in achieving success. The consensus was that a six-week Saturday academy should be implemented in every African Methodist Church. Oak Chapel plans to implement a similar program and make it available to the entire community. We must continue to facilitate spiritual growth, psychological maturity, health, and wholeness. We should not stop until all have achieved wholeness within the community.

I believe that the church as the surrogate model works because it was designed by Jesus and was built on a foundation of love. This model was open and inclusive. Jesus started out with twelve disciples and ended up with 120 people in the upper room at the point of his return to heaven. Jesus often used parables and asked questions to allow what was hindering the disciples to come out in the open. Jesus desired to help people process through their issues and move into a new level of enlightenment. His discipleship model promoted nurturing for those in this village.

Jesus used a practical theology that included healing, sustaining, guiding, and reconciling. According to the results of the pilot project, there was perceived protection for the individual in the church. The individuals did not feel that they were alone and thus did not appear to be subject to overwhelming feelings of loneliness, isolation, and alienation. In this village of care, most church members experienced love, unity, and loyalty. Most people indicated that they experienced support from the church family that positively influenced their ability to face challenges, make wise decisions, and deal with crises in their life.

The adults noticed greater confidence on the part of the young people; observing spiritual and psychological growth and maturity. There appears to be an inner security among most of the children that allowed them to believe in themselves. With hope and meaning restored, they could dream of going to college and being successful. I believe that these children and youth are like little acorns that get the necessary resources and become giant oak trees. We pray that the church as the surrogate family has provided love and the other attributes needed to counteract some of the evil influences of poverty, racism, and nihilism.

EPILOGUE

Implications and Reflections: One Experience

The church has not functioned as the surrogate family since the early church in the first century. Some churches are not much more than social clubs; others claim holiness, but all members are not holy in their actions. Some churches are involved in open sin and rebellion against God. One large denomination in the South demonstrates active discrimination against women and minorities. We believe that God is not pleased with the majority of churches.

God desires unity among his children, but the church is the one of the most segregated institutions in America. There are large mega churches that attempt to unify people from different nations, groups, and languages, however some of them have compromised the gospel of Jesus Christ. In some of those churches and ministries, the Bible does not have first priority. In that category some preach the prosperity gospel while others preach the gospel of "Feeling good and saying I love you will solve all our problems." The large churches sometimes offer a buffet of ministries, so people can pick and choose. A church buffet often leaves people without an anchor and the growing relationship in Christ that they need. The church is weak, because it is divided by denominational barriers and has strayed from the truth of the Bible.

Leaders in some denominations fight for political power within their church body while neglecting service to the poor and needy. One can determine what one values by what and where one spends time and money. God has called the twenty-first-century church to repent and return to the practices of the first-century church. After Jesus' disciples were filled with the Holy Spirit, they became unified as a body of believers. Their priorities were praying, understanding the proclaimed word of God, and sharing with one another so that no one lacked the basic necessities.

Some churches add large numbers to their rolls through evangelism but do not teach the new converts how to be disciples. They can get people to repeat the sinner's prayer, but they do not help them overcome the influences of sin, Satan, and the world. They try to put new clothes over the old, dirty ones. Salvation is instant, but discipleship must follow so that the sinful practices and lifestyle are put away. Holy and righteous thoughts and actions must replace the old ways. The majority of people have probably said the sinner's prayer but do not honor God fully with their tithes, talents, and time; being in the presence of God on a daily basis is not a priority in their daily lives.

God will soon send Jesus back on the clouds to earth to gather His church. Only those who have prepared will return with Jesus and escape the seven years of tribulation. The real church is without spot or wrinkle because it is clean, pure, and holy. There will be some real followers of Jesus from all corners of the earth. Those who have true love in their heart for God and other people will be taken into heaven to worship and praise God.

Jesus says, "But the hour is coming, and is now here, when the true worshipers will worship the Father in spirit and truth, for the Father is spirit and truth, for the Father seeks such as these to worship him. God is a Spirit and they that worship must worship in spirit and truth" (John 4:23-24). Many churches that are in existence today are lukewarm in their worship and in their works, are comfortable and satisfied with their way of life, and are not hungry and thirsty for the Word of God. Worship has become a lifeless ritual rather than real worship. Some folks never say "Hallelujah," "Praise the Lord," or "Thank you, Jesus." There is no fire in their spiritual being.

Jesus told the church at Laodicea, "I know your works; you are neither cold nor hot. I wish you were either cold or hot. So because you are lukewarm and neither cold nor hot, I am about to spit you out of my mouth. For you say, 'I am rich, I have prospered, and I need nothing.' You do not realize that you are wretched, pitiable, poor, blind, and naked" (Rev. 3:15-17). The least church should be on fire for the Lord, Jesus Christ. The real church is empowered to do the work she was called to do. The real churches move forward by faith to do the greater works as they are led by the Holy Spirit. Jesus states, "Very truly, I tell you, the one who believes in me will also do the works that I do and, in fact, will do greater works than these because I am going to the Father" (John 14:12). There is no excuse for the church to be lazy, lukewarm, and lax.

Unfortunately, many people think that they are saved because they have their name on the membership book of a local church. When I was approximately fourteen years of age, I joined the United Methodist Church in our community. I sang in the youth choir and served as president of the Methodist Youth Fellowship group. We were involved in social activities but did not have a Bible study. I was never taught how to have a personal relationship with Jesus Christ. Like many people, I thought I was a good person, was a Christian, and would go to heaven. My church activities ceased during college, and other things became a priority. I began my career in nursing, but that did not make me happy. While I was teaching nursing in a university, I went to law school at night. Upon passing the bar examination, I worked hard at establishing a career in law and became successful by the world's standards.

The successful law practices afforded me the opportunity to travel and enjoy various pleasurable activities. I became driven to be more successful and make more money so I could have longer vacations away from the stress of life.

On October 4, 1997, my life was falling apart. I attended my husband's aunt's funeral. A friend from high school preached her funeral. During the eulogy a statement was made that some of us in the congregation thought we had become successful, but we would face the wrath of God. At first I thought, "She is talking to someone else." Then in the next second, I felt what I have since called a Holy Ghost arrow going deeply into my heart. I thought, "Oh no, she was talking about me." At that moment I realized that I was lost and was a sinner. Over the next six weeks I tried to be "good" and read a Bible I had been given over twenty years before. The more I tried to be good, the more hopeless I realized that I was.

On November 16, 1997, I decided to attend a church somewhere. When I drove out to the highway, I was prompted by the Holy Spirit to call a friend's house to get directions to her church. I went to that church that Sunday and accepted Jesus as my personal savior. Over the next three years, the Holy Spirit used the pastor and some elderly saints of that church to disciple me and nurture me in the faith. During that time the Lord gave me a vision of the River of Life. At the time I saw the vision, I had not read or heard about the description of the River of Life in the Bible. As I read that section of the book of Revelation, I knew that was what I had seen. I also had a night vision of Jesus, but where his head should have been was a cross. Shortly after that the Holy Spirit spoke to me when I returned from church one Sunday, saying that I had been called to be a missionary when I was a teenager. He also confirmed that the calling of God was without repentance.

After that time I began preparing for the ministry. Within a year after saying yes to my calling, my husband, who was terminally ill with emphysema, received a bilateral lung transplant. He went from being on oxygen and requiring total care to becoming independent again. I entered the itinerant ministry tract of the African Methodist Episcopal Church (AME Church) and preached my initial sermon on September 30, 2003. I was asked several times by church officials how I got into the AME Church. I explained that before she passed in November 1997, my mother-in-law invited me to her church, saying that if I was going to be a part of her family, I would need to go to church. I explained that I had not attended any other denominational church other than the AME Church since 1986. As things were beginning to look bleak, one of the pastors on the committee said, "She preached at my church when I was on vacation, and everyone told me what a wonderful sermon she preached when I returned." He proceeded to tell the committee that he thought I would be fine. The Holy Spirit had told me before the meeting that He had a man in that room, and everything would be fine. They were hesitant to admit me to the itinerant tract because they had never ordained a white female in the Second Episcopal District of the AME Church.

The Lord prepared the way by providing me the opportunity to attend seminary while I practiced law. I also attended the AME Board of Examiners classes for over four years, and I was ordained an itinerant elder in May 2008. The journey of intercultural ministry has been challenging but most rewarding. One of my closest friends said, "It must be God because normally a poor African Methodist Episcopal Church would not accept a white pastor." My friend decided that the love of God opens doors that do not seem rational to people who look through human eyes. There is no doubt that God answers prayers and brought people into the church.

The Holy Spirit reminds me that my responsibility is to speak the truth in love, and He will draw people to Jesus, convict them of their sins, and save them. We know that God allowed a donkey to speak in order to warn the prophet. God calls men and women to preach and teach the Word of God so that people can hear the gospel and be saved. God places people in churches who are available to serve; He is constantly looking around the world for humble and faithful servants who will go and minister to people who are in need. The time before the return of Jesus is very short, and He is doing some unusual and extraordinary things. Joel prophesies, "Then afterward I will pour out my spirit on all flesh and your sons and your daughters shall prophesy, your old men shall dream dreams, and your young men shall see visions. Even on the male and female slaves, in those days, I will pour out my spirit" (Joel 2:28-29).

People may still question what a white female is doing pastoring a church in the African Methodist Episcopal denomination. I believe God prepared me to serve at Oak Chapel because he had a divine plan for the church. Intercultural appointments may be challenging, but they bring more diversity than would normally be available in a more segregated congregation. God has a special place of ministry and service in his kingdom for everyone. When God brings a person to a church, he will provide all that is needed for them to fulfill his will. When a person loves God and the people, God will make it work.

Jesus is coming back for a church that is pure, holy, clean, righteous, and blameless! He will appear in the clouds above the earth and call His saints and sanctified ones to come with Him to heaven. Those that have not followed behind Jesus on the straight and narrow path will be left behind. There will even be some preachers left behind. There will also be many people whose names are on a church membership list left behind. Jesus is not pleased with the state of the twenty-first-century church! To all churches I say, "Repent, repent, and repent again of your sins! Ask the Holy Spirit to fill you with His plan and then yield only to His leading!" Jesus is seeking and searching for churches that are "on fire for Him." He will bless those churches with all of the provisions they will need to do the work to which He has called them!

If you have never truly received and welcomed Jesus Christ into your heart, and you have not experienced the new spiritual birth, you can do so right now by sincerely praying the following prayer.

> Jesus, I know that You are the Son of God, the Savior of the world, and the open door to heaven and to life hereafter. I know that You lived a perfect life here on earth and then willingly gave up that perfect life on the cross at Calvary, so that I might have eternal life in heaven. I believe that You arose from the dead after three days in the tomb. I believe that You are now in heaven, seated at the right hand of God the Father, waiting for me to join You there after my physical death. I confess that I am a sinner and that I am in need of Your forgiveness. I want to turn away from sin. I ask You to forgive me of my sins. I believe in my heart, and I now confess with my mouth these things, and I ask You to come into my heart and into my life and be my Lord and my Savior. I will trust You, live for You, and follow You for the rest of my life. In Jesus' name, I pray. Amen.

If you prayed this prayer and believed it in your heart, find a Bible-teaching church where you can grow spiritually. Your most fulfilling days are ahead, including life hereafter with Jesus and all of the saints in heaven. May God bless you in all of your endeavors! We would like for you to call the following toll-free number and tell us about your life-changing experience, so that we can rejoice with you!

1-866-505-1264

BIBLIOGRAPHY

African Methodist Episcopal Church. *The Book of Discipline of the African Methodist Episcopal Church*. Nashville: AMEC Sunday school Union, 2009.

Allen, Richard. *The Life Experience and Gospel Labors of the Right Reverend Richard Allen*. Nashville: AME Sunday school Union, 1964.

Anderson, Eric. *Race and Politics in North Carolina, 1872-1901: The Black Second*. Baton Rouge: State University Press, 1981.

Aselage, Carey, Arlana Bobo, Aviva Meyer, Betsy Neal, Katie Parker. "Warrenton, Warren County, North Carolina: A Community Diagnosis Including Secondary Data Analysis and Qualitative Data Collection." http://www.hsl.unc.edu/phpapers/warrentonol/ whistory.htm (Accessed January 3, 2011).

Banks, Robert J. *Paul's Idea of Community: The Early House Churches in Their Cultural Setting*, rev. ed. Peabody, MA: Hendrickson Publishers, Inc., 1994.

Black, Clifton C. "The First, Second, and Third Letters of John," In *The New Interpreter's Bible*, vol. XII. Nashville: Abingdon Press, 1998.

Bonhoeffer, Dietrich. *Life Together: The Classic Exploration of Christian Community*. New York: Harper & Row Publishers, Inc., 1954.

Boyd-Franklin, Nancy. *Black Families in Therapy: Understanding the African American Experience*, 2nd ed. New York: Guildford Press, 2003.

Burge, Gary M. *The NIV Application Commentary: The Letters of John*. Grand Rapids: Zondervan, 1996.

Cao, Nanlai. "The Church as a Surrogate Family for Working Class Immigrant Chinese Youth: Ethnography of Segmented Assimilation." *Sociology of Religion* 62, No. 2 (2005): 183-200.

Carlson, Tom. Oral History about Warrenton Presbyterian Church, Warrenton, NC, 2009.

Cole, Victor Babaajide. "Mark." Ed. Tokunboh Adeyemo, *Africa Bible Commentary: A One-volume Commentary*. New York: The Zondervan Corp., 2006.

Copeland M. Shawn. "Living Stones in the Household of God." Ed. Linda E. Thomas, *Living Stones in the Household of God: The Legacy and Future of Black Theology*. Minneapolis: Fortress Press, 2004.

Cooper-Lewter, Nicholas & Henry H. Mitchell. *Soul Theology: The Heart of American Black Culture*. Nashville: Abingdon Press, 1991.

Craddock, Fred B. "The Letter to the Hebrews." In *The New Interpreter's Bible*, vol. XII. Nashville: Abingdon Press, 1998.

De La Torre, Miguel A. "Pastoral Care for the Latina/o Margins." Eds. Sheryl A. Kujawa—Holbrook and Karen B. Montagno, *Injustice and the Care of Souls*. Minneapolis: Fortress Press, 2009.

Edwards, Lonzy F., Sr. *Pastoral Care of the Oppressed: A Reappraisal of the Social Crisis Ministry of African American Churches*. Macon GA: Magnolia Publishing Company, 1997.

Eli, Quinn. *African-American Wisdom: A Book of Quotations and Proverbs*. Philadelphia: Running Press Book Publishers, 1996.

Eugene, Toinette M. & James Newton Poling. *Balm for Gilead: Pastoral Care for African American Families Experiencing Abuse*. Nashville: Abingdon Press, 1998.

Floyd-Thomas, Stacey, Juan, Floyd-Thomas, Carol B. Duncan, Stephen C. Ray, Jr., Nancy Lynne Westfield. *Black Church Studies: An Introduction*. Nashville: Abingdon Press, 2007.

Franklin, Robert M. *Crisis in the Village Restoring Hope in African American Communities*. Minneapolis: Fortress Press, 2007.

Freedmen's Bureau Convention: 1866. "Minutes," Raleigh, NC. http://docsouth.uc.edu/ncFreedmen/menu.html (Accessed January 3, 2011).

Good, Deirdre. "Truth, Gospel of." In *The New Interpreter's Dictionary of the Bible,* ed. Katherine Doob Sakenfeld, vol. V, Nashville: Abingdon Press, 2009.

Hellerman, Joseph H. *Jesus and the People of God: Reconfiguring Ethnic Identity.* Sheffield: Phoenix Press, 2007.

Hellerman, Joseph H. *When the Church Was a Family: Recapturing Community.* Nashville: B& H Publishing Group, 2009.

Holy Bible, New Revised Standard Version. San Francisco: HarperCollins Publishers, 2007.

Hunt, C. Anthony. *The Black Family: The Churches Role in the African American Community.* Bristol, IN: Wyndham Hall Press, 2000.

Johnson, Ada Strong. *An Historical Sketch of the Oak Chapel African Methodist Episcopal Church of Warrenton.* Warrenton, NC: Jennie Johnson Franklin, 2007.

Lartey, Emmanuel Y. *Pastoral Theology in an Intercultural World.* Cleveland: The Pilgrim Press, 2006.

Legeros, Mike. "Early Black Fire Fighters of North Carolina," annotated. www.Legeros.com/history/ebf (Accessed Jan 3, 20011).

Lincoln, Eric C. and Lawrence H. Mamiya. *The Black Church in the African American Experience.* Durham, NC: Duke University Press, 1990.

McQueen, Michael T. "The Teens Are Watching." Ed. Anne E. Streaty Wimberly. *Keep It Real: Working with Today's Black Youth.* Nashville: Abingdon Press, 2005.

Meek, Ginger. "Rich History of Church Source of Members Pride." *Warren Record*, August 1, 1990.

Migliore, Daniel L. *Faith Seeking Understanding,* 2nd ed. Grand Rapids: William Eerdsmans Publishing Company, 2004.

Montgomery, Lizzie Wilson. *Sketches of Old Warrenton, North Carolina.* Spartanburg, SC: The Reprint Company Publishers, 1984.

Moore, John E., ed. *John R. Hawkins High School Alumni Yearbook.* Warrenton, NC: John R. Hawkins Alumni and Friends, Inc., 1984.

Moyd, Olin. *Redemption in Black Theology.* Valley Forge, PA: Judson Press, 1979.

Mucherera, Tapiwa N. *Meet Me at the Palaver: Narrative Pastoral Counseling in Postcolonial Contexts.* Eugene, OR: Cascade Books, 2009.

Oak Chapel African Methodist Episcopal Church. Letter to the Right Reverend Bishop Frederick C. James, June 9, 1996.

Okorocha, Cyril and Francis Foulkes. "Psalms." In *Africa Bible Commentary*, ed. Tokunboh Adeyemo. New York: Zondervan, 2006.

Osborne, Grant. Ed. *Life Application Bible Commentary: 1 & 2 Thessalonians*. Carol Stream, IL: Tyndale House Publishers, Inc., 1999.

Osiek, Carolyn and David L. Balch. *Families in the New Testament World: Households and House Churches.* Louisville: Westminster John Knox Press, 1997.

Perkins, Pheme. "The Gospel of Mark: Introduction Commentary, and Reflections." *The New Interpreters Bible,* vol. VIII. Nashville, Abingdon Press, 1994.

Perkins, Pheme. "The Letter to the Ephesians." In *The New Interpreter's Bible,* vol. XI. Nashville: Abingdons Press, 2000.

Powery, Emerson B. "The Gospel of Mark." Ed. Brain K. Blount, *True to Our Native Land: An African American New Testament Commentary.* Minneapolis: Fortress Press, 2007.

Raboteau, Albert J. *Slave Religion: The Invisible Institution in the Antebellum South*, updated edition. New York: Oxford University Press, 2004.

Sampley, J. Paul, "The Second Letter to the Corinthians," *The New Interpreter's Bible,* vol. XI. Nashville: Abingdon Press, 2000.

Scott, Ian W. "Truth in the New Testament." In *The New Interpreter's Dictionary of the Bible,* ed. Katharine Doob Sakenfeld, vol. V. Nashville: Abingdon Press, 2009.

Smith, Abraham. "The First Letter to the Thessalonians." In *The New Interpreter's Bible*, vol. XI. Nashville: Abingdon Press, 2000.

Smith, Charles Spence. *A History of the AME Church.* Philadelphia: Book Concern of AME Church, 1922.

Smith, Kenneth and Ira G. Zepp, Jr. *Search for the Beloved Community: The Thinking of Martin Luther King, Jr.* Valley Forge, PA: Judson Press, 1998.

Smith, Yolanda Y. "Forming Wisdom through Cultural Rootedness." Eds. Anne E. Streaty Wimberly and Evelyn Parker, *In Search of Wisdom: Faith Formation in the Black Church.* Nashville, Abingdon Press, 2002.

Town of Warrenton. "Historic Warrenton North Carolina." http://www.warrenton-nc.com/history.shtml (Accessed January 3, 2011).

US Census Bureau. Warren County, North Carolina. November 18, 2009. http://quickfacts.census.gov/afd/states/37/37185.html (Accessed January 3, 2011).

Vine, W. E. *Vine's Complete Expository Dictionary of Old and New Testament Words*. Nashville: Thomas Nelson, 1996.

Washington, James M., ed. *A Testament of Hope: The Essential Writings and Speeches of Martin Luther King, Jr.* New York: Harper Collins, 1986.

Van Beek, Aart M. *Cross-Cultural Counseling in Creative Pastoral Care and Counseling Series*. Minneapolis: Fortress Press, 1996.

Wellman, Manly Wade. *The County of Warren North Carolina 1586-1917.* Chapel Hill, NC: The University of North Carolina Press, 1959.

West, Cornel. *Race Matters*. New York: Vintage Books, 1999.

Williams, Deloris. NC Gen Web Project. John Adam Hyman Biography. August 21, 2010. http://www.ncgenweb.us/ncwarren/afro/hyman-ja.htm (Accessed January 3, 2011).

Williamson, Lamar, Jr. *Interpretation: A Bible Commentary for Teaching and Preaching Mark*. Louisville: John Knox Pres, 1983.

Wimberly, Anne E. Streaty and Evelyn L. Parker. *In Search of Wisdom: Faith Foundation in the Black Church*. Nashville: Abingdon Press, 2002.

Wimberly, Edward P. *African American Pastoral Care and Counseling: The Politics and Oppression and Empowerment*. Cleveland: The Pilgrim Press, 2006.

Wimberly, Edward P., Anne Streaty Wimberly, Annie Grace Chingonzo. "Pastoral Counseling, Spirituality and the Recovery of the Village Functions: African and African American Correlates in the Practice of Pastoral Care and Counseling." Eds. John Foskett and Emmanuel Lartey, *Spirituality and Culture in Pastoral Care and Counseling: Voices from Different Context*. Fairwater, Cardiff: Cardiff Academic Press, 2004.

Wimberly, Edward P. *Using Scriptures in Pastoral Counseling*. Nashville: Abingdon Press, 1994.

Wright, Richard R., Jr. and John R. Hawkins. eds. *Centennial Encyclopaedic of the African Methodist Episcopal Church*. Chapel Hill: University of North Carolina Press Library. 1916 (Accessed, January 28, 2011).

Wright, Richard R., Jr., ed. *Encyclopaedia of African Methodism*, 2nd ed. Philadelphia: The Book Concern of the AME Church, 1947.